THE
FLOODS
2

Playschool

THE FLOODS

2
Playschool

Colin Thompson

illustrations by the author

RANDOM HOUSE AUSTRALIA

Random House Australia Pty Ltd
20 Alfred Street, Milsons Point NSW 2061
http://www.randomhouse.com.au

Sydney   New York   Toronto
London   Auckland   Johannesburg

First published by Random House Australia 2006

National Library of Australia
Cataloguing-in-Publication Entry

  Thompson, Colin (Colin Edward).
    Playschool.

    For children aged 8+.
    ISBN 1 74166 026 2.

    I. Title. (Series: Thompson, Colin (Colin Edward) The Floods; 2).

    A823.3

Design, illustrations and typesetting by Colin Thompson
Additional typesetting by Anna Warren, Warren Ventures
Printed and bound by Griffin Press, Netley, South Australia

10 9 8 7 6 5 4 3 2 1

The Floods' Family Tree

MERLIN
Wizard

MORDONNA
Witch

Valla
Boy - 22

Satanella
Girl - 16

Merlinmary
Not sure - 15

Winchflat
Boy - 14

Morbid & Silent
Twin boys - 11

Betty
Girl - 10

Some Quicklime College teachers

Turn to page 204 for
The Quicklime College Teachers Files.

Your teachers

Look in ANY classroom.

Most children start school when they're about five or six, even witch and wizard children. In fact, six of the seven Flood children started school at about the same age as you did. A particularly brilliant witch or wizard, however, may well start school before they are born.

Winchflat Flood, who is cleverer than a whole box of knives, began school eight months before he was born, when he was just a little tadpole. To help himself add things up more quickly, he grew an extra finger on each hand and three more toes on each foot, which is why he wears such big shoes. By the time he was born, he knew more stuff than almost anyone else in the whole world.

The children's father, Nerlin Flood, though quite clever, never went to school at all. Where Nerlin grew up in Transylvania Waters – a dark and mysterious country four weeks' ride by horseback beyond the furthest boundaries of Transylvania itself, turn left at the Valley of Doom and keep going until you pass through the Arches of Darkness – none of his relations had been to school. His family were Dirt People. They lived their whole lives in the drains beneath the city, cleaning the toilets from below and making sure everything always flowed away smoothly. The rest of the population looked down on them in every way, especially on Thursdays, when they would kneel on the pavement and shout rude words down the gratings into the drains just to make sure the Dirt People never got above themselves.

'Waste of good education, teaching them to read and write,' said King Quatorze.[1] 'I mean, they

---

[1] *The King's full title is eighteen pages long but here is a brief version: King-Nombre-Sept-À-Quatorze-Knees-And-Bumpsadaisy-The-Four-Hundred-And-Fourteenth-And-A-Half-Grand-Protector-Of-The-Haunted-Grapefruit-Keeper-Of-The-Holey-Pants-Guardian-Of-The-Square-Window-*

don't need to read anything to use a shovel and a toilet brush.'

'Exactly, Sire,' agreed his Chancellor. 'And besides, it's too dark down there to read anything anyway.'

On the other hand, Nerlin's wife, Mordonna, was a princess and had received the very best education Transylvania Waters could offer. Because she was the King's daughter, she didn't go to school with the common children. She had a special governess

---

Supreme-Cuddler-Of-The-Round-Widow-Prince-Of-Half-An-Hour-Before-Twilight-Kevin-King-Of-Cardboard-Keeper-Of-The-Dinner-Money-And-All-Who-Sail-In-Her-The-Ninth-Except-On-Tuesdays.

who lived in the palace and taught her everything she needed to know. However, because Mordonna was a princess and her governess, Claypit, was just a commoner, they were forbidden to talk to each other. This meant that, although it was always very peaceful in the schoolroom, actually learning anything was a bit difficult.

Like all clever people, Nerlin and Mordonna knew that you learn tons more useful stuff after you've left school than you do when you're there. In the years since they had eloped together and travelled the world pursued by King Quatorze's agents, Nerlin and Mordonna had gathered more knowledge and wisdom than most people ever do. Now they were brilliant at magic – and they were determined that their children would be even better. They would spare no expense when it came to their children's schooling.[2] This is why they sent their children to

---

[2] *Not that money is ever a problem for witches and wizards. If they can't find a way of stealing it, they just make it using a spell and some simple everyday ingredients like shoe polish and centipedes.*

Quicklime College – a special school for witches, wizards, goblins, elves, shamans and anyone else who can do magic, and the finest school of its kind in the world.

Their youngest child, Betty, is the exception. Betty goes to the normal human's school, Sunnyview Primary School, just down the road from where she lives at numbers 11 and 13 Acacia Avenue. Betty doesn't look like her brothers and sisters. She has blonde hair and no warts at all, and likes to do things that ordinary girls do, like baking cakes and knitting. Her cakes are normal cakes with no earwigs or cockroaches in them, and her knitting doesn't have the usual wizard's spiky thorns knitted into the cuffs.

Of course, being a witch, she can still do magic, though you can't tell by looking at her. And although she knows her parents would send her to Quicklime College with her brothers and sisters if she asked, Betty likes it at normal school – especially now that Dickie Dent is no longer there to pull her hair and tease her. She does get teased by some of the other girls for being a bit different, but it's nothing she can't handle with a bit of magic – 'pain and pimples', as she likes to call it.

Valla, the oldest Flood child, left Quicklime's with a first-class degree in blood and now goes

out to work at the blood-bank. This leaves the five remaining children: Satanella, Merlinmary, Winchflat, and the twins, Morbid and Silent. They all go to Quicklime's.

Quicklime's is hidden in a remote valley high in the mountains of distant Patagonia. It's so far from anywhere that almost no ordinary humans have ever been there or even know the valley exists. There are no roads or footpaths into the place and, as there are always security clouds spread evenly above it, it can't even be seen by satellite. It has never appeared on any maps at all.

The site was chosen because it was here that the first wizards arrived on Earth. It's a well-known fact that the original witches and wizards came from a far-off galaxy where spells and magic were something everyone could do. When they got bored, they'd get in a spaceship and fly off to another galaxy to scare and/or enchant the local population, who thought magic was magic.

Nerlin's ancestor,[3] Merlin Flood the Fifteenth, came to Earth to create a few legends for humans who, until then, had lived in caves and thought the best thing anyone could do was hit someone else on the head with a lump of wood – a belief that lots of humans still have. Unfortunately Merlin's spaceship had not been serviced properly before he left home and it crashed in a remote valley in Patagonia.

Merlin's first thought was, *Plank*, which was the rudest swear word he knew. His second thought

---

[3] *Nerlin's family hadn't always been Dirt People. Once they had ruled Transylvania Waters, but, as so often happens, treachery, revolution and badly fitting tights had led to their downfall.*

was, *This is a pretty cool valley*, and with the help of Big Magic, seven robots, a tape measure and some human peasants, he built Quicklime College.[4] This took a very long time and Quicklime's was opened for business seven hundred and fifty years ago, by which time there were quite a few witches and wizards living on Earth.

Work on Quicklime's was held up for ninety-nine years while Merlin went off to help the young King Arthur with his adventures and teach him handy household tips like how to sharpen a sword that some idiot has stuck in a rock and how to make a round table so none of his knights would feel like someone else had a more important seat than they did. What was left out of the history books was all the fights the knights had with each other because no one could tell whose seat they were sitting in. Someone would sit in the wrong place and eat someone else's dessert and

[4] *When the building was finished, Merlin turned the human peasants into upside-down blind cave fish, which still exist to this day. (This is true — when I was a boy my uncle had an upside-down blind cave fish in a tropical tank. It was pink, blind and swam upside down.)*

then the fight would start. The actual table still exists and is one of Quicklime College's most treasured possessions.

Quicklime's looks like a proper wizard school should look, with lots of very pointy towers and fancy gargles around the tops of the walls. Gargles are like gargoyles except they make a loud gargling noise all the time. The three hundred and sixty-five gargles at Quicklime's have been tuned to gargle in a slow eerie wail that can be heard from hundreds of miles away, which has led to the myth that there are giants in Patagonia, something humans believe to this day.

There are three hundred and sixty-five of everything at Quicklime's, except doors. There are only three hundred and sixty-four of them, which

means that, somewhere, there is a room without a door – though no one has ever managed to find it.

Quicklime College is more than a school, it's a way of life. And unlike normal school, you don't leave forever at the end of year 12. Quicklime's is a place you go back to your whole life. If you have a problem you can't solve, you can always find the answer at Quicklime's, either in the great library or in the brains of the professors, who have lived for thousands of years.

Very few Quicklime's students ever want to take a day off from school and, if they are sick, they usually stay in the school sick bay rather than go home. Matron has far more powers than the average witch and a list of incredible medicines as long as your arm. She even has medicines longer than your arm, ancient recipes from mythical ages lost in the mists of time, when dinosaurs roamed the world – which they actually still do in Quicklime College's valley.

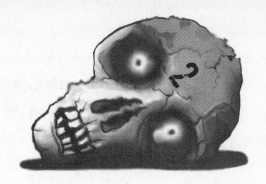

Monday morning, 8.01 am

'**S**orry we're late, kids,' said the driver as the wizard school bus arrived at 13 Acacia Avenue. 'Couldn't get the dragon started this morning. Must be the wet weather.'

Below the Floods' home at 11 and 13 Acacia Avenue was a vast network of cellars, and the bus stop was in one of these. It wasn't just the school bus that stopped there every day, but a whole range of witch and wizard transport. There were Shopping Specials that took all the mother witches to the UnderMall where they bought underwhere, extra-black eye-shadow and this season's new magical pointy objects. There were Sports Specials that took all the wizards to

intergalactic football games, and there were Holiday Specials that took the children to summer camp. All the buses were the same – not so much buses as dragons with seats and toilets, run by an interplanetary company called Blackhound. These buses travelled at a fantastic speed and there were express buses – dragons with seats and no toilets – that could travel at the speed of light. For technical reasons, which are too messy and complicated to explain, it is extremely

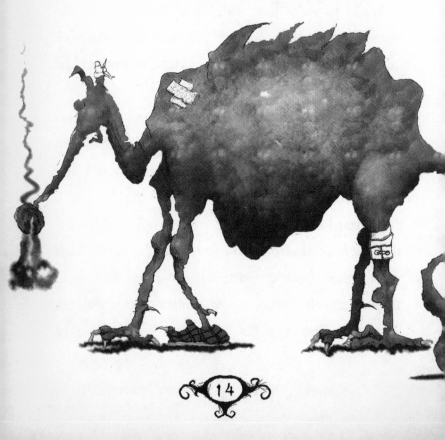

dangerous to go to the lavatory at the speed of light.

The dragon stood at the bus stop, with smoke trickling out of its nostrils. Its eyelids kept dropping shut as if it was about to fall back to sleep. It looked very old and tired, which it was. It had been taking children to Quicklime's for two hundred years and it wanted a rest. All it could think of was the school holidays when it could spend all day asleep in its cave. It should have retired years ago, but there was no one to take its place. Dragons have always been very misunderstood. Humans have never been able to see the poetry in them burning down the occasional village and carrying off beautiful women, and have persecuted them for centuries until dragons have sadly become an endangered species. The few remaining dragons are now protected by spells of invisibility so humans can never see them.

'Come on, children, we've got fifty-eight seconds to make up,' said the driver as the five Flood children climbed aboard. 'And no blood-letting in the back seats.'

Fifty-eight seconds might seem like less than a

minute, but when you travel as fast as a Blackhound school bus, that's all it takes to travel a few hundred miles.

The Flood children were the first on the bus each morning and always sat in the back row where they could see everything that was going on. Winchflat was head boy at Quicklime's, which meant he had the power to remove or seriously modify the head of any child who was naughty. He was so conscientious that he once removed his own head for twenty-four hours for accidentally tripping up a junior witch.

On a normal bus journey, it's nice to look out of the window as you travel along. On a dragon bus, all you see is blur, clouds, blur, and blur, but the journey is over so quickly there's no time to get bored. There's not even time to finish the homework you didn't do last night. Because a lot of wizard homework involves small unpleasant creatures, a fair bit of blood and slimy stuff, homework has been banned on school buses since the time an out-of-control intestine wrapped itself around the bus driver's eyes and made him crash into a volcano.

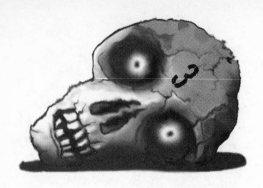

Morning Assembly
Headmaster: Professor Throat

Every morning the entire school gathered in the Grate Hall, which is not the Great Hall spelled in an old-fashioned way, but a huge room that has an enormous fireplace – the Great Grate – because it is very, very cold in the Patagonian Andes. At the opposite end of the hall, in the centre of the stage, sits King Arthur's round table.

Professor Throat stood in front of the round table and raised his hand. Gradually the children fell silent. Tame bats were put back in schoolbags. Extra heads were tucked inside shirts and light sabres were switched off. Even the school creep, Orkward

Warlock, managed to stop his right eye twitching for a few moments.

'As you all know,' the Professor began, 'in eight weeks time we have our annual sports day.'

Everyone cheered.

'Exactly,' Professor Throat continued. 'And we all know that sports day is the highlight of our school year, the only day when outsiders are invited to the school – your parents and siblings, former students dead and alive, and special guests from other worlds and dimensions. And this year, of course, is extra special because it is exactly seven hundred and fifty years since the school was opened by our glorious founder, Merlin Flood, in this beautiful valley, safe and secure in the high Patagonian Andes. So let's make this sports day the one that will go down in history.'

Everyone cheered, stamped their feet and threw stuff up in the air, including wizard hats, wands, toes, an elf called Nigel and several breakfasts.

'And now, all students please be silent for the school anthem,' said the Professor.

Unlike other schools, where everyone sings a really boring song while some dotty old lady plays on an out-of-tune piano, Quicklime's school anthem was sung in Braille. Everyone closed their eyes and ran their fingers over a card with the words embossed on it. It was the most peaceful three minutes and twenty-seven seconds of the day, just enough time for all the teachers to have a cup of tea and a biscuit.

It was hard that day to concentrate on the school anthem. The announcement about sports day was filling up everyone's head. Many children, including the Floods, had spent months preparing themselves with special training. Satanella had spent hours in the back garden of 13 Acacia Avenue chasing her tail round and round Queen Scratchrot's grave. So far she had never managed to catch it, which didn't really matter as there was no tail-chasing event in the school sports.

'Mind you,' she'd said to her brothers and sisters, 'as soon as I do catch my tail, I will petition for it to be included. I mean if they allow beach volleyball in the Olympics, they'd have to let tail chasing in.'

(Sport at Quicklime's is not like sport anywhere else. Here are a few of the best-loved events past and present:

- **Wizard Rules** – *Twenty-two players stand in the middle of a soccer field and watch as all the spectators kick a ball around the terraces. Sometimes the players get overexcited and throw things such as intestines and referees into the crowd.*

- **Gristleball** – *See the next chapter.*

- **The high jump** – *This was abandoned in 1873 after a small wizard, Obadiah Flood (distant relation), jumped up into the clouds and was never seen again. There is a small sect living in a cave near Mount Everest that is waiting for the day when Obadiah will return to Earth. They prophesy that this will be next Thursday just after lunch and he will reappear in Mexico. No one knows why they are waiting in the Himalayas.*

- **The long jump** – *Because this event took too long, it has been replaced by the short jump. The school record is 0.003 seconds.*

- **Cross country** – *In 1994, the school made Belgium so cross that everyone at Quicklime's had to wear a T-shirt for the rest of the year that said: 'Belgium is not at all boring. It is a really, really interesting place.'*

- **The pole vault** – *Temporarily cancelled because*

there is no more room in the vault and Poland has lodged a complaint with the United Nations.

- **Three-legged race** – *Teams are made up of families. Where there are more than two children, like in the Flood family, they are all tied together and have to leave some of their legs in the changing room. Where there is only one child, they are allowed to grow an extra leg for the day. There is always a protest about this race from the Millipedes – a family of witches and wizards from a damp ditch in Tristan da Cuhna – who claim the whole race is 'leggist'.*

- **Long distance cricket** – *You will probably find it hard to believe but long distance cricket is actually slower and even more boring than normal cricket. One wicket is on the school playing field and the other wicket is thousands of kilometres away in the back yard of number 7, The Street, St Kilda.*[5]

---

[5] *A very remote island off the west coast of the Outer Hebrides, which is off the north-west coast of Scotland.*

Top score for a three-day match is Quicklime College 3, Scotland 0.)

After the school anthem, other teachers stood up one by one with various announcements: things that had been lost – the usual iPods, fountain pens and fingers; and things that had been found – usually nothing because the school was kept very clean and tidy by someone we shall meet later.

And as it was the first Assembly of term, there was a report of the past holiday's great achievements by students and ex-students. The highlight that holiday had been Winchflat Flood's creation of a volcano right at the North Pole.

'Talk about global warming!' said Professor Throat to hoots of laughter.

'Well, I thought that was what they wanted,' said Winchflat. 'What with so many humans walking around whingeing about how cold they were.'

Finally, Assembly was dismissed and everyone went off to their classes. Classes at Quicklime's are different from those at other schools. Apart from the

subjects being much more interesting, children of different ages are often in the same class. Quicklime College knows that you don't get more clever as you get older. You're as clever when you die as you are on the day you're born. The only difference is that you know more stuff.

Even better, the school doesn't make anyone go to any lessons they find boring – which is a bit like a Steiner school, except that at Quicklime's everyone actually learns to read and write. So, if you are really keen on something like genetic engineering, you can go to every single Genetic Engineering class each week no matter what age you are. And if you think that maths is boring, which of course it is, you don't have to go to any Maths classes. The only rule is that you have to go to four classes every day.

The Flood twins, Morbid and Silent, went off to study Invisibility. Satanella trotted off to her Special Breeds class.

Winchflat, who was brilliant at everything, shook a little bag with all the lessons written on different tiles, like Scrabble, and picked out the class

he would go to first. His favourite class was Genetic Engineering, so to make sure he went to that class more often than the others, he had twenty-three tiles with 'Genetic Engineering' written on them and only one each for the other subjects.

And Merlinmary went off to play Gristleball.

Lesson: Sport with Pain

Teacher: Radius Leg

'Today, children, we will enjoy the pain that great sport can bring,' said Radius Leg. 'I don't mean the pain caused by the screaming boredom of watching a normal human soccer match or the pain of trying to stay awake during a normal human cricket match. Nor do I mean the mild physical pain of playing cricket with hand grenades. I mean the sheer bone-breaking, skin-tearing, blood-squirting, bubonic-plague-ridden joy of Quicklime College's own special game: Gristleball.'

The thirty-nine children in the class were standing at the top of the Gristleball field as the

school's sports teacher addressed them. They were all raring to go because, like all lessons at Quicklime's, you didn't have to go to Gristleball classes unless you wanted to. The only student who had no choice was Orkward Warlock. Orkward spent his entire life at the school, including holidays, weekends, half-term and even Christmas Day, and because he was a naturally lazy boy, Professor Throat had decided he should play Gristleball to get some exercise.

Unlike other sports, there were no different leagues for boys and girls. In fact, when the players were dressed in their protective clothing, you couldn't tell who was a boy and who was a girl.

Gristleball was not played on the normal school playing field. Because of the frequent accidents, it had its own special place away from the rest of the school in a one-hundred-metre deep three-sided pit carved into the rock. This helped to muffle the sounds of agony that accompanied every game. At the bottom of the pit sat the playing field. There was no soft girly grass and mud down here, just smooth slippery marble. On each side of the field there was a goal similar in shape and size to a football goal, except the goals were alive and could change size. Radius Leg and the players were lowered into the Gristleball pit in a wicker basket.

'Right,' said Radius Leg. 'Misery House side one, Leech House side two, and Gored House side three.'

Orkward Warlock, who was in Misery House, took up his usual position of creeping off the field and hiding in the toilets, which were in a little cave near one of the corners. He always pretended he was in there in case the gristleball came flying through the window, but everyone knew he was just scared.

Radius Leg moved to the boundary and blew his whistle. In the centre of the triangle, the ground began to shake. The marble cracked from side to side, rose up and suddenly burst open as the ballworm reared up out of its tunnel. It tipped its head back, heaved, opened its mouth wide and spat a massive ball of slimy gristle embedded with nails into the air. As the ball shot up into the clouds, the ballworm slid back into its burrow, pulling the rocks and marble

back down behind it. The players stood looking up into the sky, waiting for the gristleball to reappear.

Three minutes went by as the gristleball hovered above the clouds, waiting for the moment when the players would drop their concentration for a split second.

Merlinmary Flood loved Gristleball. Round the walls of her bedroom in Acacia Avenue she had photographs of all the greatest teams and players Quicklime's had ever produced. If it had been up to her, she would have played Gristleball every day, but it was only played once a week to allow the players time to re-grow the bits of their bodies that had broken off during the game. With her incredibly thick hair crackling with electricity, she was the only player in the history of the school who had played the game

without protective clothing. Those few minutes when the ball hid in the clouds were the most exciting moments of her life. The anticipation was almost too much to bear and it was all Merlinmary could do not to give herself a serious electric shock.

The seconds ticked by as the ball hovered. The seconds became another minute and still the gristleball waited. And then, at the very moment when the players least expected it, it came screaming down, heating up as it did so until it was glowing red. If a team was ready and in the right place, they grabbed the gristleball in their asbestos gloves and threw it into the nearest goal.

If it was their own goal they got ten points. If it was either of the other two goals they scored five. For every other player the ball crashed into, seven points were added. If it hit Radius Leg and threw him against the boundary wall, the team got fifteen points plus one extra point for each broken rib.

That day, the ball flew straight down towards Merlinmary, but she was ready. She grabbed it and, ignoring the smell of her own fur beginning to burn,

she spun round in a blur of sparks and fire before hurling it with an almighty scream. It knocked three players to the ground, smashed through the lavatory window and threw Orkward Warlock down into the toilet bowl with such force that the entire thing shattered, leaving him sitting in a pool of water with the wooden toilet seat around his neck like a huge collar.

'Goatface pig bottom!!' he screamed through his pain as the ball shot back through the window towards the opposite side of the field. For as long as

he could remember, Orkward Warlock had hated the Floods. Every day there was something else they did that made him hate them more.

Merlinmary's throw shot through all three goals before hovering just out of reach in one of the corners of the playing pit while the gristleball regained its strength. Her score was forty-one points, though when it was later discovered what had happened to Orkward Warlock another twenty-seven points and a gold star were added – seven for hitting Orkward and a special referee's bonus of twenty for smashing the toilet, which no one had ever done before. The fact that he had been the source of Merlinmary getting anothet twenty-seven points made Orkward hate the Floods even more.

The game ended when the gristleball ran out of energy. It collapsed in the corner panting for breath until Radius Leg gave it a drink of water and summoned the ballworm to take it back to its nest.

The highest score ever for a single throw had been four years before, when Valla Flood, in his final game before leaving school, had thrown the

gristleball through his own goal with such force that it had thrown Radius Leg against the wall and broken nine of his ribs before bouncing back across the field seventeen times through all three goals and finally hitting Radius Leg a second time, breaking both of his legs. The score was one hundred and eighty-seven points, more than double the previous record. It had earned Valla a lifetime honour award, fifty out of ten and a whole bucket of gold stars.

'They don't make gristle like that any more,' Radius Leg would say proudly, stroking his scars as he remembered that wonderful day.

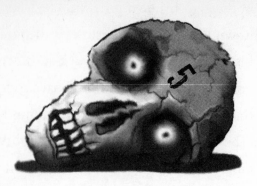

Orkward Warlock hated everyone. He hated his parents. He hated his sister Primrose, who was disgustingly nice, and he hated all the other relations he assumed he had but had never met. He hated his teachers and every other person he knew or read about or saw on TV. Sometimes, for practice, he even hated himself, and pretty well everyone hated him too.

But Orkward Warlock had one hate that was deeper than all his other hates. It was so dark and deep that it had no end, like the lake in Scotland where the Loch Ness Monster lives. This hate was bigger than all Orkward's other hates added together and multiplied by twelve plus seven.

The thing that Orkward Warlock hated more than anything in the whole universe was the Floods.

Orkward Warlock was one of the twenty-seven boarders at Quicklime's. The boarders were usually children who lived too far away to be able to come to school by bus each day. The fleet of wizard buses that took the children to and from school covered the entire globe. There was even one very small witch – Felicia McThursday – who came from a lighthouse on a remote rock fifty kilometres past Iceland. The children who boarded at Quicklime's came from even further away, from other galaxies and parallel universes.

All except Orkward. He was the only boarder who actually came from Earth, and *he* was a boarder because his parents couldn't stand to have him at home, not even during the holidays. He had spent every single day of his life since the age of three days at Quicklime's. In the holidays, when everyone, including his sister Primrose and most of the teachers, went home, Orkward stayed behind with Matron, Doorlock the handyman, George Shrub the

37

mandrake gardener and Narled, a strange creature, half man, half suitcase, who spent the whole time picking things up and taking them somewhere.

Over the years, several children and teachers had invited Orkward to come and stay with them in the holidays, but to everyone's relief he had always refused.

'I think my parents are coming to take me to Tahiti,' he would say, but everyone knew it wasn't true.

Because Orkward was at school all the time, Professor Throat had given him his own room up in one of the seven-sided turrets. It was there, in the darkness, where even spiders were afraid to go, that Orkward practised hating. Around the walls of the room, he had photographs of everyone – every student, every teacher and all the other staff – and

into these photographs he stuck pins and knives and knitting needles. Everyone knew he was doing this and wore an amulet issued by Matron that protected them against the magic.[6]

---

[6] *Radius Leg chose not to wear his amulet as he liked the sudden unexpected searing bolt of agony when Orkward stuck a needle in his photo. When Orkward found out about this, he immediately stopped doing it.*

Sticking pins into pictures of the Floods wasn't enough for Orkward. It didn't begin to cover the hatred that he felt for them. They had everything. They had brothers and sisters to play with and parents who loved them, and they all seemed to like each other. They even did smiling,[7] and their mother, Mordonna, was one of the most famous witches that had ever existed. Her beauty was legendary across the galaxies. Her photo was pinned up in cafes and bars in every one of the fifteen parallel universes. Orkward didn't even know what his own mother looked like. All he could remember about her was a blurry face close to his and a voice saying, 'Take it away, it's the ugliest thing I've ever seen.'

Nerlin, the Floods' father, as well as being a direct descendant of Merlin Flood the Fifteenth, was in *The Hemlock Book of Records* as the owner of the world's hairiest wart in the most embarrassing place. Everyone at Quicklime's thought Nerlin was a

---

[7] *Orkward had tried smiling once but his mirror had laughed at him and the whole thing had made both him and the mirror sick for a week.*

legend – even though he'd never attended the school. Orkward had no memory of his own father and no one had ever spoken of him, not even Primrose.

Primrose never spoke to Orkward about anything. It had come as a complete surprise to both of them to discover, after Primrose had been at Quicklime's for four years, that they were actually brother and sister. Orkward was one of those boys who thought girls were gross and didn't want anything to do with her. Primrose, like almost everyone at Quicklime's, thought Orkward was vile and wanted as few people as possible to know she was related to him. Orkward had tried a couple of times to befriend his sister so he could find out about their parents, but his attempts at friendship were a bit like a crocodile

trying to make friends with your leg. He just didn't know how to do normal things like smiling or being nice. In the end Primrose told him they were not related and that he had been adopted. It wasn't true, but at least it meant he stopped bothering her.

When no one was watching or listening, Orkward would lie in bed in the darkness and nearly allow himself to cry. He would imagine a gigantic white dragon arriving in the valley with the greatest wizard in creation riding on its back, a wizard who was king of all the other wizards, a wizard who had arrived for one reason and one reason only – to claim his long-lost son, Orkward Warlock.

The truth was not so wonderful. Orkward Warlock's father was a milkman, an ordinary middle-aged balding human with no magical powers and a small moustache that he called Gerald. Orkward's mother, who was a genuine witch, had only married him because she was addicted to milk and couldn't afford the fifty litres a day she needed to drink and bathe in to keep her skin glowing white.

Orkward had only two friends. One was an

innocent boy known as The Toad, who spent many hours under Orkward's bed cuddling Orkward's dirty socks. The other was a magic mirror, but that didn't really like him or tell him what he wanted to hear.

'Mirror, Mirror on the wall,' Orkward would say, 'who is the cleverest boy of all?'

'Winchflat Flood,' The Mirror would reply. 'Why do you keep asking me? You, like, totally know the answer, idiot.'

'You are, Orkward,' The Toad would call out from under the bed. But Orkward would always get so angry he would take The Mirror off the wall and stick it under the bed with The Toad.

'Mirror, Mirror on the floor,' Orkward would say, 'who has the most evil eyes?'

'Merlinmary Flood,' The Mirror replied.

'You do,' squeaked The Toad as Orkward threw a well-aimed boot under the bed.

Whatever Orkward asked The Mirror, the answer was always one of the Floods.

'Enough with the Floods already!' screamed Orkward as his brain contorted itself in rabid anger.

'I need a plan,' he said, trying to calm himself down. 'A plan to finish the Floods off once and for all.'

'Sports day,' whimpered The Toad.

'Shut up, slug pus,' sneered Orkward and threw another boot under the bed. 'Don't you need to go somewhere and shed skin?'

'You could get them on sports day,' said The Toad, crawling out to get Matron's special bruise ointment, which he always kept close by since he'd become friends with Orkward. 'It's the only day when they're all together at the same time, and it would be really dramatic and worthy of your great evil.'

'Shut up, shut up, shut up!' shouted Orkward, stamping his foot on the tube of bruise ointment. He had forgotten that he'd thrown both his boots at The Toad, and the purple ointment began to soak through his socks and dissolve his toenails.

The Toad started to lick Orkward's toes clean. The Toad lived with a terrible conflict going on inside his head. Basically he was a sweet kind child, but because he was a toad, not many people wanted to be his friend. No one at all wanted to be

Orkward Warlock's friend, so when The Toad came along, Orkward took him under his evil wing. The trouble was, there was no place for sweet and kind in Orkward's world so The Toad had to pretend to be nasty and mean like Orkward.

'Hold on,' Orkward said. 'Even though you are fifty million degrees more stupid than an amoeba, that is actually a brilliant idea. Sports day is the highlight of the year. I will make this one the sports day to end all sports days, the ultimate sports day, the sports day people will remember forever, when all the Floods will die in one magnificent, er, skull-shattering, um … something or other.'

'YES!' cried The Toad.

'No you won't,' said The Mirror glumly from under the bed. 'You'll totally stuff it up. You always, like, do.'

'One more crack from you,' Orkward snapped, 'and you'll get a million cracks with a hammer.'

'Was that meant to be, like, a joke?' said The Mirror.

'I don't do jokes,' said Orkward.

Lesson: Invisibility
Teacher: Prebender Glorious

Prebender Glorious stood in front of the class with his usual Monday morning thought crashing against the inside of his skull. The thought was: *I wish I was anywhere but here.*[8]

Prebender Glorious taught Invisibility and he taught it very badly. He himself had a habit of

---

[8] *That was the abbreviated thought and all Prebender Glorious had time for. The full thought was:* I wish I was anywhere but here, doing any job but this, preferably a job that never brought me within two miles of anyone under twenty-five. What have I done to deserve this? Did I lock the back door when I left the house? I don't have a back door. I don't even have a house! *And so on for forty-three pages.*

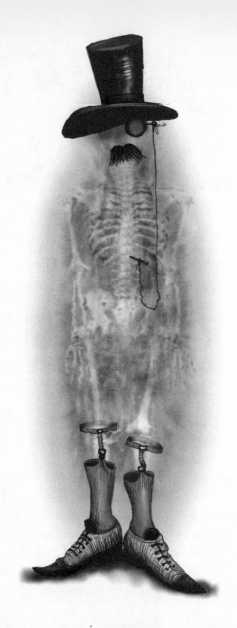

vanishing without any warning and reappearing just as suddenly.[9] It was a talent or curse he had been born with, and he had no control over it. Over the years it had brought him a lot of embarrassment, excitement, six months in prison, several million dollars and a string of failed love affairs. Sometimes just bits of him would disappear, which made going to the toilet and eating very difficult or very hilarious, depending on where you were standing.

His students, on the other hand, had mastered invisibility on their first day in the class, and now made his life hell. He sighed and took out the class register to mark everyone off.

'Portia Appleby?' There was a small pop and one of the students disappeared.

There are three children here, but they are invisible.

---

[9] *For example, if you look on pages 68 and 93 you'll see he's appeared there when he has nothing to do with the story at all.*

While Prebender Glorious looked around for Portia, Orkward Warlock leaned forward and whispered to Morbid and Silent Flood, 'You're all going to die.'

The twins ignored him. They were used to Orkward's snide remarks and knew he was all talk.

'Portia Appleby? Where's Portia?' Prebender Glorious asked.

'Right here, sir,' said Portia, appearing out of thin air.

'But I'm not,' said Bypass Noble, vanishing.

'Now, look, come on, everyone, play fair,' Prebender Glorious pleaded, on the verge of tears.

'But we're just doing what you've been teaching us,' said Portia and the whole class vanished, except Howard Tiny, who was horribly good and didn't count. Actually he did count, really well, but never got past ninety-nine before someone stuffed something in his mouth, because as well as being horribly good, he was also horribly boring.

'Oh God, Tiny, why do they always vanish and leave me with you?'

'I don't know, sir. Would you like me to do some counting?'

'No, it's all right, thank you,' said Prebender Glorious. 'You just sit there and practise your invisibility. Try and make your mouth vanish.'

'Okay, sir. Can I count quietly? It helps me concentrate.'

'If you must.'

'One, two, three, four …'

Orkward Warlock could do invisibility but he wasn't very good at it. When you are really good at it, you can see everyone else who is invisible at the same time as you are. Orkward Warlock couldn't. All he could see when the class vanished was Prebender Glorious and Howard Tiny. For all he knew, everyone else had left the room.

'Going to kill us, are you?' Morbid Flood whispered in his left ear, while Silent blew hot breath in his right. 'We're really scared,' the voice added. 'Not!'

Two very large invisible books whacked Orkward on either side of his head. For a split second

he became visible again before collapsing on the floor with his breakfast coming out of his nose.

'Nose blister scumbags!' he shouted. 'I really am going to kill you.'

He staggered to his feet and kicked Howard Tiny, who started to cry. Orkward disappeared again before he could get into trouble.

The Monday morning thought beat even harder inside Prebender Glorious's head.

'Eighty-seven, eighty-eight, eighty-nine …' Howard sobbed.

Something snapped inside Prebender. It was his third rib disappearing. He began to wish he could have a heart attack. It would be less stressful than teaching this lot, but he knew that even if he died he would still have to teach the Invisibility class. Being dead, which several other teachers were, just meant the school could stop paying your wages. It also looked very good in the school brochure.

'Ninety-five, ninety-six, ninety-sevvv …' said Howard as Orkward Warlock's invisible hand stuffed a sock in his mouth.

There were two words guaranteed to make the students visible again and Prebender Glorious said them.

'Sports day.'

The entire class reappeared and sat quietly in their seats.

'As you all know, invisibility is totally absent from sports day,' he began. 'I mean, have we ever seen any invisible sports? No we haven't, and I for one think that it's very unfair. I petitioned the board of governors. I've even threatened to take the whole thing to the Wizard Rights Commission, and I am delighted to say that this year we will have invisibility on sports days. It will be there for all to not see.'

The class cheered with delight. Maybe they had misjudged poor old Prebender Glorious.

'What invisible events will there be, sir?' asked Bypass Noble.

'Throwing the javelin, for one,' said Prebender Glorious.

'So what exactly will be invisible?' asked Morbid. 'Us or the javelin?'

'Both.'

'Wow. So how will anyone know how far the javelin's gone or even where it's gone?' said Portia Appleby.

'By the bloodstains on the grass,' Prebender Glorious explained.

'I like it,' said Orkward Warlock. 'Can we practise on each other?'

'No, Orkward, you cannot. Now we will practise our invisible maths for the rest of the lesson.'

Everyone except Howard vanished again but, as the end-of-lesson bell rang, they all reappeared.

'Right, children, homework …' Prebender Glorious began to say, but they all vanished again. 'Okay, we'll … we'll skip homework again. Class dismissed.'

54

At which point the whole class reappeared and ran out of the room, except Howard Tiny, who was lying under his desk going purple as he tried to pull the sock out of his mouth, which would have been a lot easier if his foot hadn't still been inside it. Prebender rolled his eyes and went to help him, the Monday morning thought crashing around his skull with the force of a jackhammer.

From a distance, and especially when he was sitting still, Narled looked exactly like a very old suitcase. Up close you could see he had two little stubby legs at the front, two wheels at the back and a pair of arms. He appeared to have neither eyes, nor ears, nor a mouth. Where his mouth should have been was a wide leather flap that closed with a zip. Everyone assumed that Narled was once a human who had been changed into a suitcase by a spell that had been interrupted or put on him by some particularly cruel wizard, but despite all the teachers' attempts, no amount of magic had been able to undo the spell.

All day long Narled trundled round Quicklime's picking up things. Not just rubbish, but anything

that wasn't nailed down. He scooped it up with one hand, stuck it into his mouth and closed his zip. No one knew where he took all the stuff he collected, but if you left anything lying around for more than a few minutes, Narled would appear and take it away. He seemed to arrive from nowhere, and he had a strange way of being able to give people the slip. He would turn a corner into a dead end, but when you turned after him, he had vanished. There were rumours that he had a vast treasure house somewhere in the valley where he'd stashed all the things he had collected over the past six hundred years, but no one had ever found it.

'He must have stuff that's worth a fortune,' said Orkward Warlock. 'Gold and jewels and things that have become really valuable just because they're so old.'

'Shall I follow him?' said The Toad.

'Better people than you have tried,' sneered Orkward. 'In fact, anyone who's tried was better than you, you piece of dehydrated camel snot.'

The Toad worshipped Orkward, no matter how vile he was to him. Just the fact that Orkward spoke to him made The Toad happy. He looked up adoringly at Orkward, which made the boy so angry he did the yellow oozing pimple spell all over The Toad's face. This only made The Toad even happier.

'Anyway,' said Orkward, 'we need to work out a way to kill the Floods on sports day.'

'Poison,' said The Toad.

'They're wizards, idiot. Poison doesn't work on wizards.'

'Concrete,' said The Toad.

'Shut up. Or would you like me to throw something hard and smelly at you?' said Orkward.

'Ooh yes,' cried The Toad. 'Can I have the big brick? Please, go on, go on, please, please ...'

'Paper. Get me paper and a pen,' Orkward ordered. 'We are going to write down every single possible way you can kill a bunch of wizards.'

An hour later the paper looked like this:

'I know,' said The Toad. 'You need a big explosion.'

'Shut up, shut up, shut up!' shouted Orkward, stamping his foot on The Toad's lunch. 'Actually,' he added, as The Toad licked bits of wasp sandwich off

the bottom of Orkward's shoes, 'even though you are fifty billion degrees more stupid than a fly-speck, that is a brilliant idea.'

'I know how to make explosions,' said The Toad. 'My father owns the biggest firework factory in the world and I know how to make gunpowder. I blew up the toilets when I was in kindy. That's why Professor Throat made me into a toad.'

'You mean you're a real toad?' said Orkward. 'I thought you were just a really ugly boy. Yuk, a real toad, that's gross.'

'Well, I'm not one hundred per cent toad,' said The Toad. 'Each year I get a bit less toady and a bit more humany, unless I do something really bad again. Now I'm seventy per cent toad. If I'm good for the next seven years I'll be all human again.'

'You colour-blind septic-tank bog rat,' said Orkward suddenly, and kicked The Toad under the bed. 'I was sitting on those toilets when you blew them up! I couldn't sit down for two months.'

Lesson: Special Breeds

Teacher: Miss Phyllis

The Toad placed a lily pad on his seat, sat on it and waited for the class to begin. It was his favourite lesson of the week: 'Flies and Their Place in Everyday Life'. Being a toad, he knew exactly where a fly's place was. It was inside his stomach. You might think there's not much to learn about eating flies, but if you've ever swallowed a wasp you'll know it's not that simple.

Most of the other class members were less interested in today's lesson. The dogs, for example, thought flies were just a nuisance that kept trying to eat their bones and sniff their bottoms. The cats

simply thought flies were beneath contempt.[10]

The Special Breeds class at Quicklime's was for those children who, for one reason or another, had been turned into animals. Because there was such a wide variety of animals it wasn't so much about learning things as about keeping the children occupied all day. The classes were held in one of the outbuildings because the smell could get a bit overpowering at times – especially by Friday, when the sawdust hadn't been changed all week.

Some children, like The Toad, had been turned into animals as a punishment. Lucretia De Lager had bitten the

---

[10] *Actually cats are dreadful snobs and think all other creatures are beneath contempt.*

head off the sugar plum fairy and eaten it. She had
been turned into a cat. Squire Nutkin had been
changed into a squirrel simply because he had such
an awful name.[11] Brian Lowflush had been turned
into a bird of paradise as a reward, and others, like
Satanella Flood, who was a small black dog, had been
changed by accident.[12]

    Everything was different in the Special Breeds
class. Animals know that there are a million more
interesting, exciting and useful things than learning

---

[11] *No one ever said it was easy being a wizard.*

[12] *Mordonna kept offering to turn Satanella back into a little
girl, but she had decided life was more fun as a dog. 'Of course,
if I fall in love with a handsome wizard I'll probably want to
change back,' she said. 'But on the other hand I might fall in
love with a whippet.'*

how to add numbers up.[13] Dog numbers are easy. There are only two numbers for them: 'some' and 'none'. And that's two more numbers than snails need. Of course, the teachers tried to teach the animal-kids things they thought would be useful, but statements like 'Hello, children, today we are going to learn about French verbs' were usually greeted with replies like 'Grrrr' or 'Hiss' or 'Bark off'.

In the end, they reached a compromise, which basically meant no boring stuff like Maths and Belgian and History, and lots of very interesting stuff like eating flies and spiders, catching red rubber balls and chasing small defenceless animals. Each day focused on the interests of a different type of animal and Tuesday, The Toad's favourite, was amphibians day. The favourite activity that day was playing with the dress-up box. Everyone enjoyed that, though they got annoyed when the octopus kept taking all the high-heeled shoes.

'Right, children, spider juggling,' said Miss

[13] *Except the Millipede family, who are obsessed with numbers and spend all day counting their legs.*

Phyllis. 'Now we all know what happened last week when Nigel tried to juggle six tarantulas, and I'm happy to tell you that he is now out of the coma. So this week we are going to start off by juggling ants.'

The only child who enjoyed this was Kevin Flamboyard, who had been turned into an anteater by an ant he had eaten who was a leprechaun in disguise and not an ant at all. Kevin flicked his tongue round the classroom and swallowed every single ant.

'Okay, children, moving on,' said Miss Phyllis. 'Sports day is coming up and, as you know, the Special Breeds class always puts on an event. Last year we did underwater juggling, though unfortunately we did lose a few students like Norma Jean Gorgeous the butterfly. This year we need to come up with something safe that the whole class can be in without anyone drowning or exploding. Any ideas?'

'Tail chasing,' said Satanella.

'Some of us haven't got tails,' said The Toad.

'Well, you could all chase mine,' said Satanella.

'It's an idea,' said Miss Phyllis.

'How about tying a time·bomb to her tail,'

suggested one of the rats, 'and if we don't catch it in time, it explodes?'

Satanella reminded the rat what small dogs could do to rats. In the end it was agreed that they would chase Satanella's tail around the running track but there would be no time bombs involved.

'How about a firework?' said the rat.

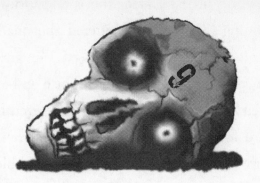

'Everyone has their price,' said Orkward, 'even a crappy old suitcase.'

'But Narled can't hear you,' said The Toad.

'I think he can,' said Orkward. 'You just watch him closely. Don't forget that I'm here in the holidays when there's no one around. I've seen him. I think he can hear and I think he can see.'

Orkward put on his silent shoes and went down into the quadrangle, where he hid behind a small tree and waited. The quadrangle was the central point of Quicklime's. Almost everyone in the entire school passed through one of its thirteen arches at some time of the day or night, including Narled.

Sure enough, fifteen minutes later, the tell-tale

squeak of his little wooden wheels told Orkward he was coming. The creature entered the quadrangle from the ninth arch, criss-crossed the grass and cobbles, picking up odd bits of rubbish and another forgotten iPod, and left through the seventh arch. Orkward followed him, his silent shoes completely silent even when he trod on a sheet of bubble-wrap containing a squeaky rubber bone.[14]

But Orkward knew that Narled knew he was there. He didn't know how, and the creature certainly gave no sign that he was aware of Orkward following him, but he knew. Orkward knew and he knew that Narled knew he knew and that Narled knew he knew he knew.

Narled went through the main gate, across the bridge over the black moat, where a class of year 5 students were being taught Underwater Japanese, and turned left along the dirt track that led down into the bottom of the valley. As he rounded a corner, he turned suddenly and slipped between two bushes.

---

[14] *Which Narled had strangely failed to pick up.*

But Orkward had seen him and followed into the dark forest that surrounded the school. When they had gone a few hundred metres into the gloom, the path ended in a small clearing and Narled stopped.

'I need your help,' Orkward said. 'I'll make it worth your while.'

Narled turned and faced the boy.

'So you *can* hear me,' said Orkward.

Narled sat back on his wheels and tilted his handle to one side. Orkward thought he saw the sides of the suitcase move slowly in and out as if Narled was breathing. He looked old and tired, as only a very well-travelled suitcase can look.

'If you help me,' said Orkward, 'I'll polish you.'

Narled's handle quivered.

'I'll polish you with the finest linseed oil and beeswax,' Orkward continued.

Narled's whole body quivered and gave a great sigh.

'All you have to do is carry a small box from A to B and leave it there,' said Orkward. 'You could do that, couldn't you?'

Narled frowned, which meant the bit of leather above his zip wrinkled a bit. He began to open his zip as if to speak, but then closed it again.

'I'll tell you what,' said Orkward. 'Just to show I mean it, I'll meet you here tomorrow and I'll bring the polish and a very soft black velvet cloth.'

Narled un-frowned, quivered, and turned away. The dark forest opened its branches and Narled trundled off into the darkness. Orkward tried to follow him, but the branches locked together again, barring his way. Although he wanted to go after Narled, he was, like all bullies, a terrible coward and was quite relieved that he could go no further.

'I'll take that as a yes then,' he said and hurried back to the college.

'Where the hell am I going to get some linseed oil and beeswax polish?' said Orkward, pacing up and down in his room.

'Matron's got some,' said The Toad, hopping back and forth out of Orkward's way. 'She put it on my back when I got sunburnt.'

'Well, go and get it, you pee bottle.'

'She won't just hand it over,' said The Toad. 'She said it's priceless, Matron's Enchanted Wax, been in her family for generations, the same magical

self-filling tin. It was given to her great-great-great-great-great-great-great-great-grandmother by Merlin himself to polish King Arthur's round table.'

'Well, go and steal it then, twit brain,' Orkward ordered.

'I don't know where she keeps it.'

'Well, go out and get sunburnt again.'

'But sunshine is banished here. You know that,' whimpered The Toad. 'When I got burnt before, it was that afternoon when He Who Must Not Be Talked About took away the clouds.'

'He Who Must Not Be Talked About?' said Orkward. 'Who the hell's He Who Must Not Be Talked About?'

'I don't know, no one ever talks about him.'

'I think you just made him up,' said Orkward, furious that he had never heard of someone so evil even his name couldn't be spoken, and so clever he could steal all the clouds. 'I've never heard of him.'

'That's because no one ever talks about him,' The Toad tried to explain.

'You just did,' said Orkward. 'Oh well, we'll just

have to improvise. Where's my massively powerful flame gun?'

'Wh-wh-what do you want it for?' asked The Toad, thinking it might be a good time to find a cold wet stone to crawl under.

'Well, if the sun won't burn you, I'll have to.'

'I'd rather you didn't,' said The Toad.

'Don't be such a baby, it won't hurt.'

'Yes it will.'

'Oh yes, so it will,' said Orkward. 'But it won't hurt *me*.'

There was a big flash, a loud scream of pain and a rather pleasant smell of braised toad.

As he carried the whimpering creature to sick bay, Orkward whispered, 'Now listen, you little slimeball. Matron will ask you how this happened and when she finds out it was me, she'll come looking for me. That's when you grab the polish and take it to our secret place, where I'll be waiting.'

'But …' The Toad began.

'Fail and I'll kill you,' said Orkward, dropping The Toad at the sick bay door and backing away.

'Succeed and you'll get a big reward.'

'Reward? Wow, what reward?'

'I won't kill you.'

Lesson: Genetic Engineering
Teacher: Doctor Mordant

octor Mordant stood in front of the class while his students settled into their seats. Genetic engineering was one of the most popular classes at Quicklime's, not just because the idea of creating new and exciting lifeforms was a lot more fun than French or History, but also because of Doctor Mordant himself. Doctor Mordant was so devoted to his subject that he constantly practised his skill on his own body. He currently had three arms, two heads and a chicken's foot, though, as everyone knew, this could change at a moment's notice.

For example, this Tuesday there was something

beginning to grow out of one of his heads that could only be described as broccoli.

'Right, class, homework,' said Doctor Mordant's left head. 'How did you all get on? Did you produce something?'

Most of the children nodded and held up their hands to be first to show their results.

'Excellent,' said Doctor Mordant's right head. 'Let us re-cap. The exercise was to take a small mammal and a piece of soft fruit, combine their genes and create a new and cuddly yet delicious lifeform.'

'You, Smeak Junior, what have you got to show us?' Doctor Mordant's left head asked.

'Well,' said young Smeak, placing what looked like a bowl of mangoes on the laboratory bench, 'I crossed a kitten and a mango. I call them Mittens.'

'But they look just like mangoes,' said Doctor Mordant. 'I see no evidence of kitten at all.'

'Try and eat one, sir,' said Smeak.

Doctor Mordant picked up a Mitten and held it to his nose.

'Smells wonderful,' he said. 'Exactly like a mango at the perfect point of ripeness.'

'Take a bite, sir.'

As Doctor Mordant opened his left mouth, there was a violent flash. The Mitten appeared to turn itself inside out and attacked Doctor Mordant's

nose with a flurry of flying claws that sent splashes of blood everywhere. As soon as the doctor dropped the creature, it reverted back into an innocent-looking piece of fruit.

'Just think of the market potential,' said Smeak, as the poor doctor dabbed at his bleeding face. 'Slip one in a bowl of fruit at a party or a business meeting – absolute chaos.'

'Brilliant,' said Doctor Mordant, who had no problem with a bit of pain and blood-letting in the pursuit of science. 'Ten out of ten and a silver star.'

The whole class cheered.

'Who wants to go next?'

Everyone looked at everyone else. Smeak Junior's Mitten had been brilliant and no one wanted to follow it.

'Come on,' said Doctor Mordant. 'Letitia, what about you?'

'Well, I've only got a photo. I had a bit of a problem,' the girl replied.

'Explain.'

'Okay, I couldn't find a mammal and Mum

wouldn't let me use the dog after what happened when I crossed the budgie with a crocodile last week.[15] So I had to use a snake and I crossed it with a tomato.'

'Well, that sounds promising,' said Doctor Mordant. 'We weren't going to use reptiles until next term, but never mind. So what went wrong?'

'I called it a Tomython,' said Letitia. 'And it looked brilliant, two metres long and bright red.'

'So where is it?'

'Well, that's the problem,' Letitia explained. 'It looked so brilliant and delicious that every time it caught sight of its own tail, it ate itself.'

---

[15] *You can imagine the chaos created by a metre-tall bird, with massively powerful jaws full of very sharp teeth, landing on top of people's heads shouting, "Who's a pretty boy then?"*

The whole class burst out laughing.

'It's not funny,' said Letitia. 'I had seven goes and it did the same thing each time.'

'And then what happened?' said Doctor Mordant.

'I ran out of tomatoes.'

'Winchflat, I'm sure you have something wonderful to show us,' said Doctor Mordant.

Winchflat Flood was not only head boy, but he was the school genius. He was one of those children who seem to be brilliant at everything. But Winchflat was different from most really clever kids who come top all the time, in that he was pretty cool and all the other kids liked him. Except Orkward Warlock,

of course. Of all the Floods, Winchflat was the one Orkward hated most.

'As you know, I've been trying to clone Clarissa, the dodo I managed to hatch out of a three-hundred-and-fifty-year-old egg,' Winchflat began. 'Well, last weekend I cracked it. I put fifty dodos aside to send back to Mauritius, where they came from, and I had a few spares.[16] So I crossed one of them with a cabbage.'

He reached into a big sack and lifted out his creation – the Dabbage. It was even uglier and more ungainly than a dodo. It had two short fat legs and a big lumpy beak, but instead of feathers it had green cabbage leaves. The creature hopped down from Winchflat's desk, waddled across the room and fell over.

'That's useless,' sneered Orkward Warlock.

---

[16] *Merlinmary Flood is trying to train some of Winchflat's spare birds as homing dodos. They're very good at finding their way back but, because they can't fly and are rather fat, they can only find their way home from about two hundred metres away. Merlinmary is now trying to teach dodos to read maps.*

Winchflat just smiled.

'And what did you make, Orkward?' Doctor Mordant asked.

'Umm, well …' Orkward began.

'Bring it out here, boy,' said Doctor Mordant.

Orkward put a matchbox on the teacher's desk. Doctor Mordant peered inside.

'A baked bean? You made a baked bean?'

'No,' said Orkward. 'I crossed a baked bean with a flea.'

Before Doctor Mordant could ask him why, the baked bean leapt out of the matchbox and began hopping around the room. The class erupted as everyone tried to catch Orkward's Flean. The Mittens and several other creations popped out of their fruity forms and scrambled out of the way, but some were trampled underfoot. The Parrotato flew out of the window through the narrow bars and landed on the grass as a pile of chips with feathers, and the Bunion[17] crawled up Doctor Mordant's trouser leg.

In the midst of the chaos the Dabbage plodded quietly around the room eating all the squashed experiments. It all ended when the great creature opened its beak and the Flean hopped right down its throat. The Dabbage let out a dreadful green belch, which made everyone's eyes water. It then jumped on top of the smallest child in the room, Howard Tiny, and tried to hatch him out.

---

[17] *A cross between a bat and an onion.*

'Calm down, class,' said Doctor Mordant, turning towards the blackboard. 'Let's move on. This week's homework is to take a herring and an accountant and swap their brains over.'

'Why?' said Orkward.

'Good question, er, er …'

'Orkward Warlock,' said Orkward.

'Yes, Orlock Warkward,' said Doctor Mordant. 'The point of the experiment is to release our modified fish and accountants back into the wild and see if anyone can tell the difference.'[18]

'And of course,' he continued, 'I trust you are all working on your creatures for sports day. Last year we produced the Centithlete, a creature with one hundred legs that could outrun the fastest sprinter. Let's see if we can do better this year.'

'I have one,' said Orkward.

'Really, um, er, Orkflit. Do tell.'

---

[18] *It should be noted that this experiment had been done three hundred years earlier by Doctor Mordant's predecessor and that most of the accountants currently alive do actually have fish brains.*

'A Tyrunningosaurus,' said Orkward. 'Not only will it run faster than everyone else, but it will eat them all as well.'

'You haven't actually made one, have you?' asked Doctor Mordant nervously.

'No, sir. It's just an idea.'

'Well, I think maybe it's a bit too violent,' said Doctor Mordant.

'I have another one, sir,' said Orkward. 'You take all the sand out of the short jump pit and fill it with piranhas.'

'Yes, er, thank you, Orwhat.'

Doctor Mordant and Winchflat carried the Dabbage down to the front office and duplicated it on the Special 3D Photocopier that Winchflat had recently invented to clone his pet dodo Clarissa, before releasing the two of them on the edge of the dark forest. There, they evolved into the Giant Green Patagonian Condor that we all know and fear today. Because Winchflat had the only surviving creature in Genetic Engineering that week, he got ten out of ten and a gold star.

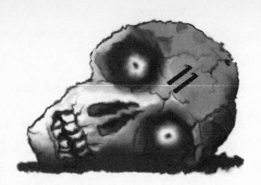

Back in his room, Orkward thought about He Who Must Not Be Talked About while he waited for The Toad to be treated in sick bay. Maybe his daydreams were true. Maybe He Who Must Not Be Talked About was the great wizard on the white dragon – his father.

'You are, like, so pathetic,' said The Mirror, which could read Orkward's mind.

'I'll smash you into a million pieces, you recycled milk bottle,' Orkward snarled between gritted teeth.

'No you won't,' said The Mirror.

'Give me one good reason why not,' said Orkward.

'One? I can give you three.'

'What?'

'Three, you little loser,' said The Mirror. 'One: I am seriously powerful and magic and, like, totally unbreakable. Two: you are a pathetic coward and wouldn't dare.'

'Why are you always so awful to me?' asked Orkward.

'Well, there are three reasons. One: you totally deserve it. Two: it's my job. And –'

'What's the third reason?'

'If you hadn't interrupted me, I was just about to say,' said The Mirror. 'Three: because I enjoy it.'

'No, no, no. What's the third reason why I won't smash you into a million pieces?'

'Ahh, that one. Well, the third reason is that I know who He Who Must Not Be Talked About is.'

'Who? Who? Tell me. Tell me!' shouted Orkward.

'Maybe I will and maybe I, like, won't,' said The Mirror.

'Tell me NOW or I'll smash you into a million pieces!' screamed Orkward.

87

'Oh man, we have totally been through that already. You can't smash me into pieces, remember?'

'Tell me,' said Orkward and, gritting his teeth and crossing his fingers behind his back so it wouldn't count, he added, 'please.'

'Well, well,' said The Mirror. 'Nice. I didn't know you could do nice, even if you have got your fingers crossed behind your back and don't really mean it. Still, it's a start.'

'Are you going to tell me?'

'Probably, but you have to do something for me.'

'Okay,' said Orkward. 'What?'

'Clean me and hang me back up on the wall so I can see out of the window again.'

'All right.'

'You have to do it before I tell you, because I think you're going to be, like, totally disappointed,' said The Mirror.

Orkward dragged The Mirror out from under the bed, hung it back on the wall and began to dust it with a square of frayed black velvet – the security blanket he had wrapped round his thumb when he went to sleep for as long as he could remember.

'You've missed a bit,' The Mirror said seventeen times before finally adding, 'Cool, now I can see right over the rooftops and into the totally dark forest.'

'Okay, who is He Who Must Not Be Talked About?'

'The chairman of the school governors, Councillor P.J. Plausible,' said The Mirror.

'What a ridiculously implausible name,' said Orkward. 'So why is he called He Who Must Not Be Talked About?'

'I don't know. No one will talk about it. I do know he took the clouds away for an afternoon as a punishment because he said the school was going soft.'

'Now I'm really depressed,' said Orkward. 'I'll have to go and hurt something.'

'I know something else,' said The Mirror, 'but it will cost you more than you can afford.'

'What?'

'He Who Must Not Be Talked About is not your father, but I know who is.'

'I don't believe you,' said Orkward.

'Fair enough,' said The Mirror, staring out of the window at the Giant Green Patagonian Condors circling over the forest.

'You don't really know, do you?'

'Oh yes, I, like, totally do,' said The Mirror.

'Tell me … please.'

'Absolutely, no problem,' said The Mirror. 'Just pay my price and I'll tell you straight away.'

'What's your price?' Orkward asked with a dreadful sense of foreboding.

'It's no big deal. You just have to, like, get me something from Narled's treasure trove.'

'But no one knows where it is,' said Orkward.

'Someone does.'

'Who?'

'Narled.'

'Yes, but, I mean, oh God,' said Orkward, slumping down in his chair and putting his head in his hands in total despair. He desperately wanted to know who his father was, but hundreds of people had tried to find Narled's treasure trove, and no one had succeeded. There were rumours, of course, and two students had actually disappeared while searching for it. Another had tried to follow Narled into the dark forest and come back as a sad electronics salesman forever lost in a never-ending quest for a larger plasma television than anyone else had ever seen. Someone had even come back Belgian.

'But what do you want it for?' he added. 'You're a mirror.'

'How many other talking mirrors have you, like, met?' The Mirror asked.

'Well, erm, none actually.'

'Exactly. I might totally look like a mirror. I might even, like, totally be a mirror, but I used to be a man.'

'Really?'

'Yeah man, really,' said The Mirror. 'I used to be this really cool handsome rich dude.'

'So what happened?' said Orkward.

'Oh, you know, the usual story. Some wizard dude fancied my girlfriend but she was, like, totally in love with me and wouldn't have anything to do with him. So he turned me into a mirror. Actually he turned me into a lobster but agreed to change me into a mirror if my girlfriend said she would marry him.'

'Why a mirror?'

'Well, the wizard dude threatened to cook me in a rather nice parsley sauce and my girlfriend said she would be his if he would spare me, and the wizard dude said okay, he would change me into a mirror so he could admire his reflection in me every day.'

'So how did you end up here?'

'Long story, way too complicated,' said The

Mirror. 'But there was a lot of blood and tons of celery involved. I don't want to talk about it, man.'

'I still don't see how Narled's treasure will help you,' said Orkward.

'The wizard dude thought my girlfriend would eventually fall in love with him, but when she didn't he turned her into a china doll. One day he put her down on the grass for a moment and the next moment, Narled had picked her up and taken her away. And, like, the thing is, if we are put together again, we will totally change back into our real selves.'

'Oh, wonderful,' sneered Orkward. 'The love story of the century – a nasty mirror and a china dolly. Hooray.'

'Fair enough,' said The Mirror.

'No, no, I'm sorry,' Orkward lied. 'I'll try.'

'This is, like, such a totally pointless exercise,' said The Mirror. 'You couldn't find your way out of a paper bag, never mind track down Narled's legendary treasure trove.'

'Yes I can,' said Orkward. 'I'll come up with a plan.'

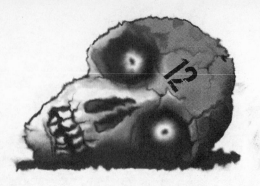

The Toad lay face-down on a bed in sick bay while Matron rubbed her legendary linseed oil and beeswax into his burnt back. Although Matron looked remarkably like a small concrete shed, she had a heart of gold and the children at Quicklime's adored her. She had two assistants, Nurse Romeo and Nurse Juliet, who were two large black crows that could sew skin together with stitches so delicate they were impossible for the human eye to see. Because of the physical, hands-on nature of a lot of the classes and some of the unusual sports at Quicklime's, this was something they did every day. They were also expert at taking people's temperatures with the thermometer in places that could make your eyes water.

'How did this happen, dear?' Matron asked. She had a soft spot for The Toad, having patched him up so often.

'I'd rather not say, Matron,' said The Toad. As the wonderful Enchanted Wax soaked into his skin, the pain slowly faded until the poor toad felt himself floating away in a cloud of turpentine.

'Were you playing with matches again?'

'No, Matron.'

'You weren't up to your old firework-making tricks again, were you?'

'No, Matron. I have toad's feet, remember?'

said The Toad, adding wistfully, 'I can't even light matches any more.'

'Someone did this to you, didn't they?' asked Matron gently.

The Toad didn't answer.

'It was that vile Orkward Warlock, wasn't it?' said Matron. 'It's all right, you don't have to say. It's obvious. You just lie there and rest while I go and get the nasty little devil.'

As soon as Matron had left, The Toad climbed down off the bed, grabbed the tin of wax and made for the door.

'Where do you think you're going, sunshine?' said Nurse Romeo.

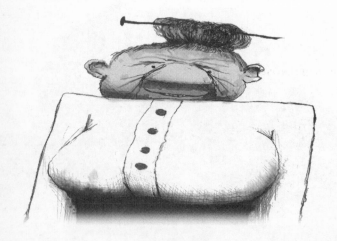

'I'm better now,' said The Toad. 'I should get back to class.'

'And what do you think you're doing with Matron's Enchanted Wax?' said Nurse Juliet.

'Umm, oh, I must have picked it up by mistake,' said The Toad, reaching for the door handle behind his back.

'Put it down.'

'I'll just, erm, er, take it to Matron,' said The Toad. 'She might need it.' And he ran out the door.

As the two nurses flew after him, he managed to hide behind a statue and give them the slip. When he was sure there was no one about he made his way to the secret place up in the thirteenth clock tower,[19] where Orkward was waiting for him.

'Brilliant,' said Orkward. 'You're almost useful. Now get lost.'

---

[19] *The school has thirteen clock towers because, unlike the rest of the world, Quicklime's runs on a twenty-six-hour day. Each tower rings on its own hour with a different note so that wherever you are in the valley you always know what the time is to within fifty-eight minutes (each hour has fifty-nine minutes).*

'Can I come with you?' said The Toad. 'I could carry the polish.'

'I suppose,' Orkward agreed. If they got caught at least he could blame it all on The Toad.

It took a while to slip out of the school without being seen, but finally they reached the path in the dark forest where Orkward had spoken to Narled the day before.

'Right, we sit here and wait,' said Orkward.

'Do you really think he'll come?'

'Yes,' Orkward replied with great confidence. He didn't actually think Narled *was* going to come, but sure enough a few minutes later there was a rustling in the bushes and there he was.

He was not alone.

There was another suitcase creature with him, slightly smaller than Narled, and around their feet were six little handbags.

Orkward and The Toad were speechless.

Narled was not, as everyone assumed, the result of an experiment gone wrong, but a real animal. *Sacculus Pluscruris Patagonius* was a very rare

species of creature that only survived in the safety of Quicklime's remote valley. Once, similar species had lived on every major continent but they had been hunted to extinction everywhere except for this one place. Their skins had been made into suitcases and holdalls, and even their babies had been made into little bags and purses. Nowadays suitcases are usually made of nylon and plastic, but in the past, the more endangered the animal, the more desirable was the luggage.

'I've … I've, er, got the polish,' Orkward mumbled as the tiny handbags ran between his legs.

The Toad sat down and reached out to stroke them. One of them climbed onto his lap and nuzzled into him. It smelled of warm leather and brought a lump into The Toad's throat that stirred up a feeling he'd spent the last few years trying to forget. When he had blown up the toilets and been turned into a toad as a punishment, his parents had been unable to accept it. His father had rejected him instantly and his mother, although she had tried really hard to keep loving him, had found it impossible to pick him up and cuddle him ever again. Since then, he had spent every school holiday in a pond at the bottom of his

parents' garden with a lot of toads who were real toads and really, really stupid.

Now this little handbag's affection brought it all back and The Toad felt tears welling up in his eyes. He tried to hide them. He knew how Orkward would sneer at him and, as horrible as Orkward was, he was the closest thing The Toad had to a friend. But two more of the tiny handbags climbed into his lap and The Toad couldn't stop himself.

He wept uncontrollably.

The first handbag opened itself, took out a tissue and handed it to The Toad. This kindness only made

him cry more. Narled's wife came over and patted him on the arm. She undid her zip, took out pen and paper and wrote: 'We feel your pain. We are here for you.'

What had made the near extinction of their species even sadder was that *Sacculus Pluscruris Patagonius* had finely tuned emotions, much finer than ours, that could not only pick up other creatures' feelings, but get inside their heads and discover the reasons for those feelings and then respond in a deep and meaningful way.

Meanwhile, Orkward was so obsessed with his plan that he noticed none of this. He was too busy polishing Narled and pretending to be his friend. Of course, being super-sensitive, Narled didn't believe a word of what Orkward was saying, but hey, he was getting the best polishing he'd had in a hundred years.

The delirious smell of turpentine seeped through the little gaps in his zip and into his brain, where it brought back long-buried memories of centuries past when every suitcase family had had a faithful servant who had polished them every day. Even in those days Matron's Enchanted Wax had been legendary, the finest polish of all, which only the most noble suitcases were allowed to use. Thoughts of the past and its former glories filled his heart with sadness. How had it come to this, a life of picking up after those who had once been their servants?

'Right,' said Orkward. 'It's agreed. I will bring you a small package and you will take it to the Floods when they are in the middle of the stadium next week on sports day.'

Narled wrinkled up, and Orkward took this to mean that Narled would do what he wanted, but Narled was just wrinkling his skin to make sure the polish got right down into his creases.

'And to show how much I really, really like you,' said Orkward, who had just thought of another plan, 'I'll come back tomorrow and polish you again.'

Mrs Narled, or Narlene as she was known to the rest of the cloakroom,[20] handed The Toad another piece of paper: 'Don't be a stranger.'

And the family trundled off into the dark forest.

'I expect you're wondering why I said I'd come and polish that suitcase again,' said Orkward, completely unaware of The Toad's unhappiness. 'Well, I have an absolutely brilliant plan.'

The Toad said nothing. All he could think of was going back and being with the baby handbags.

---

[20] *Just as you get a flock of sheep and a pride of lions and a lump of PE teachers, so you get a cloakroom of* Sacculus Pluscruris Patagonius.

'Listen,' Orkward raved on. 'I'm a genius – more of a genius than that idiot Winchflat Flood! Next time I polish Narled, I'm going to fix a tracking device to his straps, then the idiot will lead us straight to his treasure.'

'Oh,' said The Toad as they walked back to the road.

'Wait,' said Orkward. He took a jar out of his pocket, scooped a big lump of polish out of Matron's tin and put it in the jar.

'You better take the Enchanted Wax back,' he said. 'I'm going to hide this here in the bushes for next time.'

'I think I'll just creep up and leave it outside Matron's door,' said The Toad. 'She's a bit formidable when she's angry.'

Lesson: Economics and Other Forms of Burglary

Teacher: Aubergine Wealth

The two strongest boys in the class stood behind Aubergine Wealth, who was stuck in the doorway, and pushed. This was always happening, not because he was too fat, but because he had so much money, his wallet wouldn't fit through the door.

'Thank you, boys, and a gold star to each of you for stealing my gold watch and signet ring without my realising it,' he said. 'Today, we will continue working on our plan to remove all the gold from Fort Knox, but first I'd like Morbid and Silent to give us their report on how they got on "borrowing" the Crown Jewels from the Tower of London.'

Morbid and Silent went to the front of the class. They were each wearing a priceless crown. Morbid was carrying the royal sceptre and Silent the golden ball.

'Well, as you can see,' announced Morbid, 'we achieved our goal.'

The rest of the class, except Orkward Warlock, cheered. The only treasure Orkward had ever managed to steal was a jar of marmalade from the school kitchen. Although he was useless at theft and international money laundering, and consistently failed Aubergine Wealth's class, this was not really Orkward's fault. When the boy had been sent to the school at the age of three days, his parents had paid Quicklime's headmaster, Professor Throat, NB, PDF, PS, to cast a spell that made it impossible for Orkward to leave the valley. The last thing they wanted was their beloved son turning up unexpectedly.[21]

'We also got this,' said Morbid, dragging a chair out from behind a cupboard. 'King Edward's coronation chair.'

Silent grunted and proudly held up the chair, which had a small pink cauliflower sitting on it.

'Oh yes,' Morbid added. 'We also got a bonus –

---

[21] *Orkward's parents tried not to think about the day their son would finally leave school and return home with his nasty little head full of revenge. 'We'll blow that bridge up when he comes to it,' said his mother.*

a prince's brain.'

'Oh, well now,
I'm not sure that was such a
good idea,' said Aubergine Wealth.

'Well, sir, we thought that too. So we put it
back, but no one could tell the difference, so we
thought, what the hell, and kept it.'

'No, no,' said Aubergine. 'That's not what I
meant. The reason I said it wasn't such a good idea is
that it's not really worth anything, is it?'

'Actually, sir,' said Morbid, 'we've had seven

bids for it on eBay. It's up to seven hundred dollars so far.'

Silent was so excited that he nearly spoke. Not that anyone could tell, though later on when they got home Silent handed his twin a piece of paper, which said: 'I got so excited today I nearly spoke.'

'Ah! Now that, boys and girls, is what this class is all about – enterprise and the unbridled joy of making lots of money,' said Aubergine Wealth. 'Well done the Flood twins, ten out of ten and two gold stars.'

Orkward was livid. It seems that whatever the lesson was, the wretched Floods always got top marks and a gold star. He could feel the veins in his head beginning to throb and that meant only one thing. As soon as he possibly could, he would have to kick someone smaller than he was.

All The Toad could think of was going back to Narled and his family. Matron's polish could wait. While Orkward was busy hiding his jar and marking the spot with some twigs so he could find it again, The Toad went round a bend in the path and hid behind a tree. A few minutes later Orkward went by and The Toad walked back into the forest.

When he reached the place where he'd first met the family, it was deserted, but the branches that had parted to let Narled's family through were still open so he followed the path into the darkness. Instead of closing him out like it had with Orkward, the forest opened its arms to him. The branches moved aside, welcomed him in, then closed gently behind him.

The ground was covered with the little footprints and tiny wheel tracks of Narled's family. Here and there other paths crossed the main one, and they too were covered with the same marks, but The Toad kept walking straight ahead.

He had never been into the dark forest before and didn't know anyone who had, student or teacher. Even Orkward Warlock, who spent the whole of every holiday at Quicklime's, had never been any further than the closed branches. The entire forest was out of bounds, and even to wizards and witches it was an ominous and terrifying place, a kind of impenetrable nightmare that surrounded the entire school. There were those who thought the dark forest was not a forest at all but some huge living creature.

The Toad was the sort of animal who always thought the best of everyone. If someone hit him over the head, he would admire the stick they had hit him with. It simply didn't occur to him that things could be deliberately bad or unfair. When he'd been turned into a toad – which was a very, very extreme punishment for accidentally blowing up a few toilets,

especially considering that the only injury caused was a nasty burn on Orkward's bottom, which everyone agreed the boy deserved – even then he hadn't complained.

'I suppose I deserve it,' he had said, flicking a fly off the ceiling with his tongue. 'You know, I'd never realised just how delicious flies were,' he added, looking on the bright side.

Now as he walked deeper and deeper into the gloom, it simply didn't occur to him to be scared. After all, why would anyone want to harm him? He was just a little toad.

'Hello?' he called out from time to time, but there was no answer.

Dinner time came and went. The dark forest grew darker and The Toad began to falter. His little legs had been aching for a while but he had been so intent on his mission he hadn't noticed. He turned a corner, tripped over a tree root and fell flat on his face.

'Oh well,' he said to himself. 'Seeing as how I'm already lying down, I might as well have a little rest.'

He curled up in some wet leaves. In seconds he was fast asleep.

Lesson: Elocution[22] and Howling
Teacher: Mademoiselle Fifi la Venus

The noise was deafening. The entire class was howling, screaming and wailing at the top of their voices, not in harmony like a choir, but each student practising his or her own specialty.

This was the only subject that Orkward Warlock was any good at. He could scream with such a piercing whine that he could make goldfish explode, and often did. He hoped today's class would be focusing on screaming.

Mademoiselle Fifi la Venus held up her wings and waited for the class to quieten down. They

---
[22] *Talking proper.*

didn't, so she fluttered up to the ceiling and opened her mouth. Instantly, before she could utter a sound, everyone stopped in mid-scream. They all knew only too well what could happen when the Mademoiselle shouted. Almost every child in the class had had at least one eardrum transplant in Matron's sick bay.

'Right,' said Mademoiselle Fifi la Venus, 'now we have loosened up our voices, we will begin today's lesson. Orkward, get a cloth and wipe the goldfish off the back of Howard's head.'

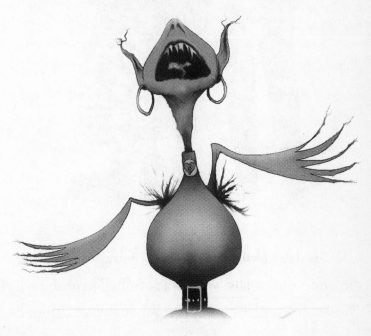

Orkward didn't so much wipe Howard's head as push it down inside his shirt and jacket. Howard started counting to himself, which he always did when it got dark suddenly.

'Today, children, we are going to practise throwing our voices,' the Mademoiselle continued. 'We've all learned how to throw our voices around

the valley without losing them. Except you, Howard. How is your new voice, by the way?'

'It's a bit odd, miss, fourteen, fifteen, sixteen,' squeaked Howard. 'Every time I speak, I think it's someone else talking. What? Who said that?'

'Well, until you find your own voice again, you'll just have to make do with that one.'

'Yes, miss. What, twenty-seven, twenty-eight?'

'Be quiet, Howard,' said the Mademoiselle.

'I didn't say anything, miss. Did I? What, forty-three?' Howard squeaked.

'Now, class, we are going to learn to throw our voices further away.'

'Are we going to practise on goldfish?' Orkward asked.

'Shush please, Orkwood. By the end of term I want every one of you to be able to throw your voice back to your own home. I want you to be able to say something to your parents from the other side of the world.'

Orkward Warlock felt a lump coming into his throat. Not only had he been sent away from his own

home at the age of three days, he didn't even know where that home was. He had a terrible feeling that he was going to cry and had to bite his lip so hard it bled. The absolutely, totally, completely last thing he ever wanted was for any of the other children or teachers to see him cry. Pretty well everyone knew he cried quite often and they thought they should feel sorry for him, but because he was so horrible, they absolutely, totally, completely wouldn't. Except The Toad, who thought Orkward was wonderful, even if he did keep exploding the goldfish The Toad was about to eat for lunch.

'We are going to aim to all throw our voices at the same place. First, we will practise with harmonised humming. When we've mastered that, we'll go on to throwing actual words. Follow me,' she said, pointing to a map of Patagonia and beyond. 'We will aim south and all focus on this point here in Antarctica.'

The twenty-seven children and their teacher began to hum in perfect synchronisation. Softly and low at first, then gradually rising in volume and

pitch until they sounded like a single high-pitched ear-splitting scream. The windows began to vibrate and then shattered, not into hundreds of pieces like a normal high note would do, but into a fine dust that blew away in the wind.

A line of trees in the dark forest shivered, shedding leaves as the voice, now too high for normal ears to hear, climbed up the side of the valley and over the mountains towards Tierra del Fuego. The sound tore a furrow across the sea as it flew towards the South Pole and finally reached the exact point that Mademoiselle Fifi la Venus was pointing at on the map.

The ground shook and cracked as a massive shelf of ice broke free and began to float north.

'Merlinmary, you threw your voice the furthest last week, so would you like to take over?' the Mademoiselle asked.

Merlinmary went to the front of the class and put her finger on the map, which, because of all the electricity she generated, began to smoulder around the edges. She moved her finger north and, as she did

so, the greatest iceberg in history moved north too and began to rotate.

Faster and faster it spun, creating a wider and wider circle of waves. By the time it reached the

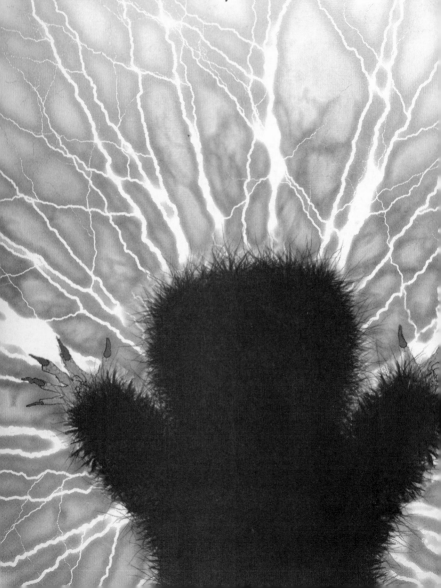

Equator, the iceberg was spinning so fast that it rose up in the air. Without the sea to hold it back, it flew with incredible speed towards Africa. The class's humming followed it, gradually turning into screaming that shook the wallpaper off the classroom walls. When the flying iceberg reached the middle of the Sahara desert, Merlinmary held up her arms and everyone stopped screaming.

Bolts of lightning leapt from Merlinmary's fingertips and flew around the room. They shot up the chimney, taking the blazing log fire with them, and up into the sky. Clouds, heavy with impending rain, exploded into steam as the lightning raced across the ocean towards the iceberg. Merlinmary clicked her fingers, shorting out the circuit, and the iceberg exploded.

It shattered into a million pieces that came crashing down into the desert, narrowly missing some very surprised camels.

The only people to see it were a team of geologists who were about to ruin the beautiful desert by drilling for oil. When they tried to tell the world about an iceberg the size of fifty football fields falling out of the sky, they were recalled to Texas and locked up in a very secure hospital, though no one ever came up with an explanation of why fifteen penguins and a seal were found wandering about in the middle of a desert.

'Merlinmary Flood, that was fantastic,' said Mademoiselle Fifi la Venus. 'Ten out of ten and a gold star.'

'Ten out of ten and a gold star, nah, nah, nah,' Orkward Warlock muttered under his breath and kicked the smallest girl in the class on the shins.

'Gold stars, gold stars,' he cursed to himself as he went back to his room to kick The Toad. 'You'll see a million gold stars on sports day!'

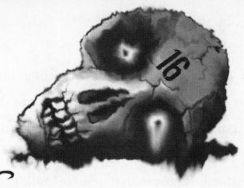

'Where on Earth am I going to get a tracking device?' Orkward said to no one in particular.

'Well, you're not clever enough to, like, build one,' said The Mirror.

'Shut up, shut up,' said Orkward.

'The only person who could build one,' The Mirror continued, 'is Winchflat Flood, and I happen to know that he's actually made one before to keep track of his sister Betty when she was a baby.'

'Shut up, shut up, shut up!'

'I'm sure he'd lend it to you,' sneered The Mirror, 'seeing as how you like him so much.'

'Hippie lavatory brain,' said Orkward and wrote a rude word on The Mirror with his greasy finger.

The door flew open and Matron marched in, followed by Romeo and Juliet.

'There you are, you evil little boy,' she said. 'I want to see you about burning The Toad, but first of all I want you to tell me where he is. He ran away with my Enchanted Wax and I suspect you had something to do with it.'

'I don't know what you're talking about,' Orkward lied.

'We'll see about that,' said Matron, grabbing

Orkward by the ear and dragging him out the door. 'You need to visit the sick bay, my boy,' she added.

'But I'm not sick,' Orkward protested.

'I know that,' said Matron, 'but you're going to be.'

As well as all the ordinary medicines like aspirins and sticking plasters, Matron had a whole range of special wizard and witch remedies. As she dragged Orkward along, the boy tried to put a spell on her. He muttered the ancient French spell that turns people into a pig's bladder, and the deadly Welsh spell that makes you wear a hat with a torch on it and sing dreadful songs for weeks on end, but Matron was immune to everything. He even tried the spell that no one realises you're doing because it sounds as if you're sneezing – the famous spell that turns you inside out. But Matron had seen every spell that had ever been invented, and had inoculated herself against all of them. She had even come up with some pretty wild spells of her own.

'You might as well stop all that,' she said. 'Far better wizards than you have tried. Okay, Nurse

Romeo, I think we'll give him a spoonful of cough medicine first.'

'But I haven't got a cough,' said Orkward.

'No, of course you haven't. That's why we're giving you cough medicine, to make you cough up the truth.'

Nurse Juliet poked her beak in Orkward's right ear while Nurse Romeo pecked the top of his head on the other side.

'AHHHHOOOWWWWWWWW,' Orkward cried and, as he did so, Matron tipped a glass of cough mixture into his open mouth.

'We'll just give that a minute to start working,' she said. 'Though, come to think of it, nasty little liars like you sometimes need a second dose.'

So the nurses attacked him again and Matron gave him another lot. It was disgusting – not just the awful taste, which was like a cross between strawberries and cow manure, but the terrifying feeling it sent through Orkward's brain. It was as if every closed door inside his head was suddenly thrown wide open and he knew that no matter how hard he tried to

fight it, he would tell the truth to whatever question he was asked.

'Where is The Toad?' said Matron.

'I don't know,' said Orkward. 'The last time I saw him, he was on his way here to bring back your wax.'

'Well, he never arrived.'

'It's the truth,' Orkward whimpered. 'Honest.'

'I can see that,' said Matron. 'Well, let's start from the last time you saw him.'

Orkward didn't want to tell her about going into the forest to polish Narled, but every time he stopped telling the truth, he began to cough, not just a bit of cough like you get with a cold, but a deep down cough that brought up his breakfast and bits of last night's dinner.

'We were in the forest …' he began.

But the last thing he wanted was for anyone to know he had been to see Narled. So gritting his teeth, he tried to lie.

Cough, bacon, cough, carrots, cough …

'You went into the forest?' said Matron. 'You know that's not allowed, don't you?'

'We were only a tiny bit in,' said Orkward. 'No more than a hundred metres.'

'And that's where you saw The Toad for the last time?'

'Yes. He set off back here, just before me.'

'You stayed behind to bury a jar with some of my stolen wax in it, didn't you?'

'No, I …'

Cough, banana, cough, carrot, splutter …

'I, er, didn't …'

Cough, porridge, cough, shoelace,[23] and then Orkward collapsed on the floor.

'Yes,' he whispered.

'Right,' said Matron. 'That's enough for now. Get into bed and rest while the cough mixture wears off. We'll talk about punishment for you burning him later. And don't go bothering Winchflat in the other bed. He's resting his genius brain. He was splitting

---

[23] *Shoelace???*

the atom all morning and then invented an anti-gravity engine after lunch, and he's totally exhausted. I don't want to hear a sound from you. You can stay here while we go and find The Toad.'

Matron locked her patients in and went to see Professor Throat. The thought of anyone, never mind an innocent like The Toad, being out in the dark forest all night, was very worrying. The two nurses flew around the school asking everyone if they had seen the poor creature.

No one had.

'And I'll tell you something very unusual,' Prebender Glorious told them with a sigh, 'I haven't seen Narled either. It's probably a coincidence, but he *always* checks the quadrangle at the end of lessons without fail. Seventy-five years I've been here, and every single night I've looked out of my window and seen him making a final check round the place before dark.'

After school, Professor Throat gathered everyone in the Grate Hall. The fire that burned in the Great Grate had been alight since Quicklime's had been built seven hundred and fifty years ago. Doorlock the handyman was the fifteenth generation of his family to care for the fire, and not once in all that time had the fire ever died. Even in summer when the temperature in the remote Patagonian valley soared up as high as five degrees, the fire was kept alight. Generations of children and teachers had been warmed by its magical flames and hypnotised by the dancing elves that lived in its fiery heart.

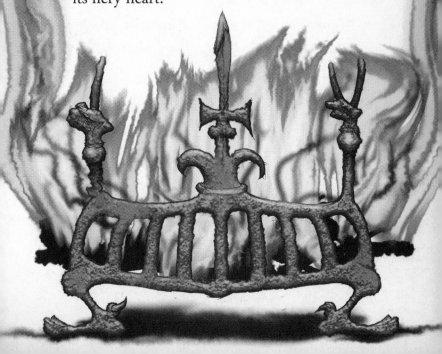

Among the staff and students, there were dozens of witches and wizards who could send their thoughts out into the world and find things.

This was how the school had become so immensely wealthy – so wealthy that it didn't have a bank account in Switzerland, it actually owned Switzerland, though they kept very quiet about it. Quicklime's economics teacher, Aubergine Wealth, had sent his thoughts out into bank vaults to look over people's shoulders when they were putting in the secret numbers to open combination locks. Then, when everyone was asleep, he sent his body over to join his thoughts and robbed them all blind.

'I only do it for a great cause,' he confided in Professor Throat. 'I am robbing the rich to help the even richer … us.'

There was only one place in the whole world where no one could send their thoughts, and that was into the dark forest.

Everyone sat very still and concentrated. The fire in the grate burned down to ash, almost dying before Doorlock came in with armfuls of fresh logs.

The school buses sat impatiently in the quadrangle and around the world parents began to wonder what was keeping their children.[24] Night fell in an enveloping silence while everyone searched the world high and low for The Toad. At midnight the children were all sent home and the staff made one final search.

'He has to be in the dark forest,' said Professor Throat.

He began to feel rather guilty. Maybe turning the boy into a toad had been too harsh a punishment. Maybe it had driven him over the edge. Though one thing didn't quite add up.

'What I don't understand,' he said, 'is that *if* he is in the dark forest, how did he get there? We all know it locks its branches against anyone who tries to enter.'

'Not everyone,' said Matron. 'Orkward Warlock

---

[24] *Quicklime's parents never worry when their children don't come home, for two reasons. One, the kids are witches and wizards so they can look after themselves; and two, Quicklime's students often stay behind at school for strange midnight ceremonies and rituals.*

told me that Narled went into the forest. He said it opened its branches for him and then closed them again before they could follow him.'

'You can't believe anything that boy says,' said Prebender Glorious.

'You can when he's had a dose of my cough mixture.'

'Ahh,' said Prebender Glorious, remembering his own childhood at the school and Matron's formidable pharmacy. 'So maybe Narled has taken The Toad.'

'I've never heard of him collecting children before,' said Professor Throat. 'It's usually iPods and socks and bits of paper.'

'And quite a lot of unfinished homework,' Doctor Mordant laughed. 'We've all heard that excuse, haven't we?'

'Yes, yes,' said Professor Throat, 'but never children.'

'But he isn't a child, is he?' said Matron. 'He's a toad.'

'I know. I know,' said the Professor. 'But I don't

think Narled has ever taken any sort of living creature before.'

They talked into the early hours and decided that at first light they would cover the valley from top to bottom to see if they could find The Toad or any way of getting into the dark forest.

When he looked back later, The Toad was never sure which bits of that night had been real and which bits had been a dream. It had been too wonderful to be real, but then it had been too wonderful to be a dream too. The Toad's dreams usually involved hopping across a very, very wide road very, very slowly while a huge truck with fifty massive black tyres hurtled towards him going very, very fast.

The last thing he remembered that he knew was real was tripping over a tree root.

Lots of little arms lifted the sleeping toad gently off the damp leaves and carried him deeper into the forest. He remembered voices like babies talking, voices that seemed to be inside his head, twittering

baby talk that didn't make words, just joyful twittering noises. And he remembered feeling happier than he had ever felt before.

Then he was in a cave on a bed of soft grass and the six baby handbags were curled up around him and their mother was singing softly to send them all to sleep. And the song was there inside The Toad's head, stroking his brain and washing away his sadness. And when the handbags were all asleep with their tiny thumbs stuck in their zips, Narlene beckoned The Toad away to the far side of the cave, where there was food and drink.

'You have a good heart,' she said to The Toad, though the words seemed to appear inside his head.

'Can you all speak?' he asked. 'Even Narled?'

'Only creatures with kind hearts can hear us,' said Narlene. 'That evil scheming boy you were with will never hear us.'

The Toad began to pour his heart out to her. He wanted to tell her what Orkward was up to. He wanted to tell her how his parents had rejected him and how big the lonely thing inside him felt, but he hardly said more than a few words before he fell asleep.

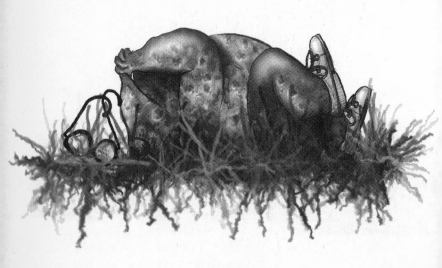

When Orkward woke up it was dark. He couldn't believe his luck. Here he was with Winchflat Flood, the one person he needed more than any other. The trouble was, Winchflat knew he hated him and he knew that Winchflat knew he knew. If Orkward was to persuade the boy to give him the tracking device, he would have to come up with a damn good plan.

Winchflat was still sleeping.

Orkward began to cry. Winchflat stirred but did not wake up. Orkward cried a bit louder.

'Who's that?' said Winchflat in the darkness.

'Oh, it's nobody,' sobbed Orkward.

I recognise that voice, thought Winchflat. *It's that vile Orkward Warlock.*

'Is that you, Orkward?' Winchflat asked, and, pretending he didn't know otherwise, he added, 'No, it can't be. Orkward Warlock would never cry.'

'Well, of course, the old Orkward Warlock never ever cried,' said Orkward, 'but things have changed.'

Naturally Winchflat did not believe a word of this. No one would, except maybe the poor innocent Toad, but he decided to pretend he did, to see what the vile boy was up to. He was just glad it was pitch dark so Orkward couldn't see him grinning.

'Really?' said Winchflat.

'Yes,' Orkward sobbed. 'It's my dear little sister Primrose. She keeps wandering away and I'm frightened that something awful in the dark forest might kill her.'

'Oh dear, that's terrible.'

'What I need is some sort of tracking device, so I can always tell where she is,' said Orkward.

'Well,' said Winchflat, 'by an amazing coincidence, I've got one. I built it when my sister was a toddler. She kept wandering off too.'

'Really?'

'Oh, yes. You wouldn't believe how far she'd go sometimes,' said Winchflat. 'Once we found her right up the top of the Eiffel Tower. Another time she was three hundred feet under the sea in the ladies toilets in the lost city of Atlantis. You know, I've always thought it was very strange that Atlantis was a lost city. I mean, how could anyone lose a whole city, and what on Earth were they doing taking it to the bottom of the sea in the first place? Then another time, we'd looked everywhere and she was right at home inside the fridge eating raspberry and rodent yoghurt. And then –'

'Yes, well. How interesting,' said Orkward, gritting his teeth to stop himself from saying something sarcastic. 'So, er, do you still use it?'

'Oh, no. It's sitting on a shelf in my workshop,' said Winchflat. 'Would you like to borrow it?'

YES! said Orkward inside his head. *God, you're dumb. I don't know why anyone would call you a genius.*

'Gosh, could I?' he said out loud.

'No problem,' said Winchflat. 'I'll bring it to school on Friday.'

After I've made a few slight modifications, Winchflat thought.

As soon as the sun rose the next morning and the wizard buses had dropped all the students back at school, groups of teachers and children set out to look for The Toad.

Radius Leg, the sports master and therefore the fittest member of staff, took a team of the older boys to the foot of the White Widowmaker, a sheer cliff of ice at the top of the valley. There was no way The

Toad could have ever climbed the Widowmaker, but Radius Leg was one of those short little people who liked to show off how macho he was.

Of course, any of the boys with him could have flown to the top of the cliff in a few seconds. They were wizards, after all. But Radius Leg said there was to be no magic involved. While he struggled up the deadly ice-face with ropes and climbing equipment, the boys sat under a tree and listened to their iPods. They knew that within fifteen minutes, their teacher would come crashing to the ground and they would have to carry him back to Matron to get mended. It happened all the time. There were enough bits of metal holding Radius together to build a small car.

'Why don't we just leave him here this time?' Morbid Flood suggested. 'Every time we carry him back to get fixed up he weighs more and more.'

Silent nodded vigorously.

'We could always sell him to a scrap metal dealer,' said one of the other boys.

Sure enough, seven minutes later Radius Leg came crashing to the ground. He lay there happily groaning in pain for another seven minutes and then fainted. The valley where Quicklime College lay hidden was the highest valley in Patagonia and the White Widowmaker was at the top end of the valley. Its sheer face sealed them off from the outside world. The air was thin and barely a day passed at that altitude without a serious blizzard.

The boys helped their unconscious teacher by relieving him of his extra weight, taking all the money and caramel toffees out of his pocket. Then they took one last look at him just to make sure he wasn't regaining consciousness, and left.

Within a few hours they were back at school warming themselves in the Grate Hall. They'd

informed Professor Throat of the sports teacher's position, but as winter wasn't that far away and Gristleball wouldn't be played again until next Easter, it was decided to leave him there.

'He'll thaw out in good time,' said the Professor. 'He always does, and it'll save the school a bit on food. You did mark his position with a stick, though, didn't you, just in case?'

Up the mountain, Radius Leg, now buried under a fresh fall of snow, began to hibernate. It was not the first time this had happened. Nor would it be the last.

Satanella Flood led a team of small animals down into the drains beneath the school.[25] This was exactly the sort of place you might expect The Toad to go – warm, dark, and dripping with slime. There were a lot of strange creatures down there who were also warm,

---

[25] *Actually, only one of them, Audrey the hamster, was a real animal. The others, like Satanella, had once been children.*

dark and dripping with slime. Most of them were the descendants of Doctor Mordant's failed experiments that had been small enough to flush down the lavatory. These creatures had grouped together, fallen in love and given birth to even stranger creatures. Their leader, Scarcely, a cross between a roller-skate, a goblin and a paperclip, was one of the blessed few with the power of speech. He and Satanella were old friends.

'No, my dear,' said Scarcely. 'Haven't seen the

little chap down here. Not for a long time. Nice little fellow, he is.'

'Well, if you hear anything, send me an email,' said Satanella.

'Can't, I'm afraid,' said Scarcely. 'Little Scrubby has eaten the modem and my niece has eloped with the mouse.'

Back in his room, Winchflat had made his modifications to the tracking device so it now had a tracking device tracking device. While Orkward Warlock would be able to track Narled once he had fitted the first bit to his straps, Winchflat would also be able to track Orkward with a third bit linked to the second bit Orkward would be using to track Narled.[26]

He then began his own search for The Toad.

---

[26] *If this seems rather complicated and leaves you feeling a bit muddled, take five minutes to run your head under a cold tap before reading any more.*

His search was through cyberspace, through the twenty-seven million chatrooms and five hundred million deadly boring blogs that five hundred million deadly boring people posted every day in the mistaken belief that it would make them any more interesting or somehow help them get a life. The Toad was not in any of these places.

It might seem weird to think the poor creature could have got trapped somewhere in the internet but Winchflat knew only too well that it could happen. Two year earlier his best friend at Quicklime's, Eric Ordinaire, had vanished into a chatroom dedicated to very early computers that could add nine and seventeen at the speed of a dead snail going backwards, and Eric had never been seen again.[27]

'I can safely say,' Winchflat later reported to Professor Throat, 'that The Toad is not in the internet.'

'How comforting,' said the Professor. 'It's a

---

[27] *If you look at the back of this book there is a page about the Mobius Strip which explains how this happens. Once you get in, you can never get out again.*

great relief to know we can cross that off our list. He probably isn't in any of the jam jars in the school kitchens, either.'

'Would you like me to go and look, sir, eighty-six, eighty-seven, eighty-eight?' said Howard Tiny.

'I don't think that will be necessary, Howard,' said Professor Throat.

'Well, he could be, sir,' said Howard. 'I mean, you could get a toad inside a jam jar quite easily, ninety-three, ninety-four, ninety-five.'

'You're absolutely right, Howard. Off you go to check. And take your time, just in case he's hiding under a slice of pickled beetroot,' said the Professor, who, like everyone else, preferred it when Howard Tiny was somewhere else.

The Toad was not in any of the jam jars. Other places he was not included the peanut butter jars and the pickled onion jars but, just to make sure, Howard took the top off each jar, stuck his fingers in and poked around in case The Toad was trapped under a large strawberry or an onion. Then, starting on the top shelf, he counted every jar, which made him so

excited he completely forgot why he was there. So he counted all the jar lids, and finally counted all the letters in all the words on all the labels on all the jars.

It was three weeks before anyone saw him again.[28]

Merlinmary Flood decided to see if The Toad was up any of the chimneys. Quicklime College

---

[28] *Apart from the kitchen maid, who came in to get some marmalade.*

had three hundred and sixty-five chimneys and Merlinmary knew a lot of them like the back of her hand.[29] Some of the chimneys didn't lead up to the outside, and although they were above fireplaces they were definitely not meant to have fires in them. These chimneys were actually tunnels that led to other tunnels that turned and twisted and joined together through the thick stone walls of Quicklime College, ending up in secret places that were so secret no one knew about them. Some tunnels were dead ends. Some were deliberate traps[30] and most of them had not been visited for centuries.

Even the teachers did not know these chimney tunnels existed. They had never felt any desire to crawl around inside dark airless places full of soot, but Merlinmary had. She had discovered the tunnels completely by accident when she had climbed up one for a dare.

---

[29] *The back of Merlinmary's hand was very hairy, which none of the chimneys was. Actually, there was one secret tunnel that was extremely hairy, but that's another story.*
[30] *The Mobius Strip again.*

While her friends stood and watched, she had crawled into the fireplace in the fourth year common room, reached up and vanished into the darkness. An hour later when she hadn't returned, her friends had begun to get worried, but they had been too scared to tell anyone in case they got into trouble. Seven hours later, Merlinmary came in through the door just as her friends had decided they better report her missing after all.

'You'll never guess where I've been,' she said.

She went back into the fireplace, but none of her friends was brave enough to follow her.

Merlinmary's tunnel had taken her out of the school, beneath the dark forest – she knew she was beneath the dark forest by the thick roots growing through the tunnel roof, roots that had moved aside to let her pass – and up into the mountains that surrounded the valley. She had been so deep inside the mountains that there was no signal on her mobile and she had been unable to SMS her mother and say she wouldn't be home for dinner.

Finally, there had been a beam of light at the

end of the tunnel and she had come out into a huge cave full of treasure. She had found Narled's legendary treasure store.

Hiding behind a pile of gold coins, she had watched as the suitcase had come into the cave, undone his zip and taken out the odds and ends he had collected that afternoon. Everyone at Quicklime's talked about Narled's storehouse and tried to guess where it was. Merlinmary was the only one to have found it, but instead of telling anyone, something told her it would be better kept secret.

Merlinmary went through all the tunnels and secret places that she had visited before – she knew there were other places still to discover – but The Toad was in none of them.

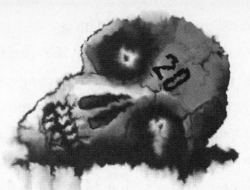

atron and the two nurses woke Orkward
Warlock up and gave him some more cough
medicine.

'Right, you little beast,' said Matron, 'take us to
where you last saw The Toad.'

Orkward shook his head but the medicine
was starting to take effect and he coughed up some
gravy.

'That's better. Now, we know you went into
the forest,' said Matron. 'So just take us to the right
place.'

'But I'm not supposed to go in there, remember?'
said Orkward. 'You said that.'

'It's a bit late for that. The forest was the last

place you saw The Toad. So that is where we are going to start looking,' said Matron.

Orkward wanted to keep the place secret, because that was where he was planning to fix the tracking device to Narled, but Matron's cough mixture had broken stronger and braver boys than Orkward and five minutes later, still dripping gravy from his nose, he was leading Matron and the nurses out of the gates and down the track to the gap in the bushes.

'Stay here,' she commanded. 'Nurse Juliet, make sure he doesn't move. Nurse Romeo, come with me.'

They followed the path until it ended in the small clearing. It was deserted apart from a gentle snoring noise coming from a pile of soft grass. Matron pushed the grass to one side and there, fast asleep with a peaceful smile on his face, was the little toad.

'Charlie,' said Matron, because that was The Toad's real name before he was changed into an amphibian. 'Time to wake up.'

She turned to Romeo. 'Just fly back and make

sure the Warlock boy is still there. Then you and Juliet take the little horror back to school and don't let him know I've found Charlie. I have a plan.'

She picked the sleeping toad up and slipped him into her apron pocket. Back in her private room, she tucked him up in bed, locked the door and told Professor Throat to call off the search.

Meanwhile, the two nurse crows had flown Orkward back to the Naughty Dungeon and locked

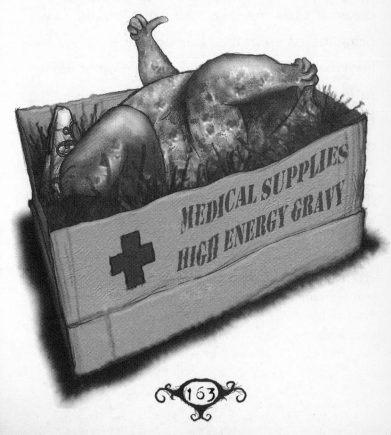

MEDICAL SUPPLIES
HIGH ENERGY GRAVY

him in there. The Naughty Dungeon was a virtual dungeon in the cellars of Quicklime's that no one had ever managed to escape from, because it was down a very, very long tunnel that led deep into the Earth.[31] It was haunted by horrograms, which are like holograms only very, very frightening. The nicest place in the Naughty Dungeon was inside the toilet bowl with the lid down.

The only thing Orkward Warlock had been better at than any other child in Quicklime's was being locked up in the Naughty Dungeon. He had been there seventeen times and was almost beginning to like it. He loved watching horror movies, and horrograms were like the best horror movies, except they leapt out and slapped you in the face when

---

[31] *The cellars beneath Quicklime College are even more extensive than the ones beneath the Floods' houses at 11 and 13 Acacia Avenue. There is a rumour that the two sets of cellars are somehow joined together even though they are on opposite sides of the planet. There is a more incredible rumour that Quicklime's cellars actually spread out like a fine cobweb beneath the entire planet. This is completely ridiculous and completely true.*

you were least expecting it. He watched them as he crouched in the toilet bowl with the lid resting on his head, but the horrograms still got him.

'That evil boy is up to something,' said Matron. 'We need a mole to find out what.'

'Well, we don't have a mole,' said Professor Throat. 'We only have a toad.'

'Well, what about if we got a mole and disguised it as a toad?'

'Hmm. Go on …'

'I think you'll agree that little Charlie has been a toad long enough, so I suggest we change him back into a little boy and hide him somewhere for the rest of the term,' said Matron. 'Then we disguise someone else as The Toad so he can find out what Orkward is up to.'

'Excellent idea,' said Professor Throat. 'Do you have someone in mind?'

'I do.'

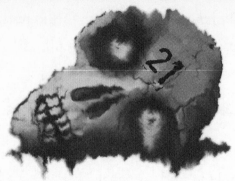

21

When The Toad was safely hidden away, Matron sent Orkward back to his room, where the pretend toad was waiting for him. Orkward Warlock never looked closely at anyone except himself, and the mole that Matron had disguised as The Toad fooled him completely.

'Where did you get to?' he asked.

'I just fell asleep in the dark forest,' said The Faketoad.

'What about Matron's Enchanted Wax?'

'I left it outside the sick bay door. Nothing to worry about. No one saw me.'

'Excellent,' said Orkward. 'Maybe you're not such a little cretin as I though you were.'

The Faketoad beamed with happiness just like the real Toad would have done.

'And look,' Orkward continued. 'I even conned that idiot Winchflat into lending me his tracking device. We'll go back to the forest and fix it onto Narled. By the end of term we'll be incredibly rich and all the Floods will be dead.'

'You're a genius,' said The Faketoad.

'It'll end in tears,' said The Mirror, who could tell instantly that The Faketoad was not the real Toad, but hadn't the slightest intention of telling Orkward.

The Mirror had seen Orkward in tears more than anyone else had. The whole school knew Orkward Warlock was a sneaky little coward, but only The Mirror knew just how big a baby he was. The boy was even scared of his own shadow.[32]

As soon as it was dark, Orkward and The Faketoad crept out of school and back to the path into the dark forest. The Faketoad was worried that Narled might be able to see that he wasn't the real Toad and give him away, but he was counting on the fact that Narled and his family liked the real Toad and hated Orkward.

Orkward collected his hidden jar of Enchanted Wax, went into the clearing and waited. Soon Narled appeared. He was alone and, as Orkward polished his leathery suitcase skin with his left hand, he fixed the tracking device to Narled's straps with his right.

'Now,' said Orkward, 'here is the package I want you to take to the Floods on Saturday. They'll win the three-legged race. They always do, the cheating

---

[32] *If you had a shadow that kept creeping up behind you and hitting the back of your head, you'd be scared too.*

168

warthog bottom bristles. When they're getting their gold medals for the three-legged race, leave the package under the winner's stand. You don't actually have to give it to them. Understood?'

Narled zipped the package away and nodded slightly.

As Orkward left the clearing, he deliberately by accident dropped a large gold coin on the path and, sure enough, Narled trundled over and picked it up before vanishing back into the dark forest.

Back in his room, Orkward Warlock turned on the tracking device base station and looked at the screen. There it was, the little blue dot that told him exactly where Narled was. The blue dot came back out of the dark forest and moved further up the valley along the road that passed the school.

'Come on, let's go!' Orkward said to The Faketoad. 'He's on his way to the treasure store, I know he is!'

They waited until they saw Narled pass by the school and then followed him at a safe distance so he wouldn't sense they were there. Eventually the

blue light stopped moving and, as they rounded a corner, they saw Narled standing completely still in the middle of the track. Suddenly he darted between two rocks – but Orkward saw him and followed.

'I've been up this road dozens of times,' he whispered to The Faketoad. 'I wonder why I've never seen this path before.'

The rocks slid together behind them, cutting off their escape.

'*That's* why,' said The Faketoad. 'Now we're trapped.'

'We'll worry about that later,' said Orkward. 'Come on.'

The path went back into the dark forest, getting narrower and steeper until Orkward was almost mountain climbing. The rocks were far too steep for The Faketoad's little legs. Maybe if he had been the real toad he could've hopped up, but The Faketoad was scared he might fall backwards.

'I think I'll just wait here,' he said, but Orkward was too far ahead to hear and besides, he had no intention of sharing the treasure with The Toad.

I wonder how Narled got up there, The Faketoad thought to himself.

Orkward came out above the trees and continued to climb. There was no sign of Narled, but he knew he was on the right track. Higher and higher he climbed until at last he reached a wide ledge at the foot of a sheer cliff. Far below him he could see the thick green blanket of the dark forest, and right in its centre was Quicklime College. Behind him was a cave, not just any cave, but Narled's secret treasure cave.

Orkward squeezed through the narrow opening and almost fainted. The cave was massive and, although the entrance was no bigger than half a doorway, the whole place was filled with light. It danced and sparkled in a million reflections as it revealed shelf after shelf of priceless gold and diamonds, and there was more – much, much more. Wherever Orkward

Warlock looked there was treasure, enough to make him the richest person in the world, richer than Aubergine Wealth, and no one knew it was there.

No one except The Toad and Narled.

So they would both have to die.

Orkward scrambled down the path to where he had last seen The Toad, but he was no longer there. He ran back to the two rocks by the road, climbed over them and raced back to the school.

'Seen The Toad anywhere?' he said as casually as he could to anyone he passed, but no one had.

Of course, the real Toad was not The Toad any more. He was now back as himself, a small boy called Charlie, and he was safely hidden away in Matron's own apartment, eating cake and wondering how much lemonade he would have to drink before he finally got the taste of flies out of his mouth.

The Faketoad was not a fake toad any more either. The Faketoad was Satanella Flood once more, and was sitting in Professor Throat's office reporting everything that had happened.

'It was brilliant,' she said, running round in

circles chasing her tail. 'The stupid boy never saw through my disguise for a moment, though I nearly gave myself away when I tried to sniff an interesting lamppost and fell over.'

'You've done very well, my dear,' said the Professor. 'Here, have a gold star.'

'He's going to try to kill us all,' she growled, finally catching her tail and biting it. 'Oww,' she added. 'That makes your eyes water.'

'Don't worry, my dear,' said Professor Throat. 'Narled has everything under control.'

As it began to get dark, Orkward gave up his search for The Toad. He took a backpack of food and a sleeping bag and hurried back up the mountain to the cave. He felt nervous being away from all that treasure, and from the ledge he could see right down into the sports field. He would stay there until the Floods were dead the next day, and then take the treasure and leave the wretched valley forever. He

knew Professor Throat's spell stopped him leaving, but he figured with a big bag of gold, he'd be able to bribe one of the dragons to smuggle him out. Even if Narled or The Toad did give him away, he would be far away.

He was just about to zip up the sleeping bag to go to sleep, when he realised that there was a better use for it. He spent the rest of the night feverishly gathering up the most valuable items from the cave into the bag, until it was bulging at the seams.

Sports Day

The school car park – which wasn't actually a car park because there were no cars parked there – was packed. Every single Blackhound dragon bus on the planet was there. Even ancient dragons had been brought out of retirement to bring all the parents, brothers and sisters and grannies to Quicklime College for sports day. Alzhammer, the oldest dragon of all, had been fitted with a pacemaker and bottled gas, and even then he'd had to set out two months earlier than anyone else to get there on time.

The stadium was packed too. Mordonna and Nerlin Flood sat in the stands beaming with pride. Betty Flood sat between them, thinking that maybe

life would be more fun at Quicklime College than it was at Sunnyview Primary School. It was something she would have to discuss with her parents.

Mordonna's mother, Queen Scratchrot, had been dug up from the back garden for her annual treat. Since the previous year most of her remaining eye had rotted away, but she didn't mind. Leaving her coffin and going out for the day was excitement enough. As the day wore on, the Queen would begin to dissolve into a puddle beneath her seat and have to be put into a glass jar, where she kept tapping on the lid and shouting because she couldn't hear what was going on, though this was probably more due to

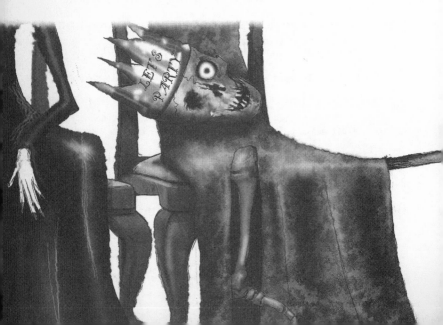

the fact that her ears had fallen off than because she was inside a jam jar.

The opening ceremony was, as always, spectacular. The children marched round the field singing the school song which, unlike the anthem, is sung at full volume.[33] When they reached the first chorus, seven hundred white doves were released into the air. Fabulous black clouds gathered over the school. Thunder roared and seven hundred bolts of lightning in perfect synchronisation fried the doves to a crisp. The delicious smell of roast pigeon that filled the air made everyone really hungry and the school cafeteria sold thousands of dollars worth of hot chips, Deadwood Dogs, and the deep-fried mini-gristles that are the droppings of the ballworm.

At Professor Throat's invitation, Mordonna Flood walked out into the middle of the field and held up her arms. All the fathers in the audience instantly  sat up straighter and began shouting, 'Take them off! Take

---

[33] *See the back of the book for a few verses of the school song.*

them off,'[34] and all their wives began hitting them with their programmes. Ten more bolts of lightning flew down from the clouds and touched Mordonna's fingertips before racing round the stadium giving everyone an electric shock – something that wizards and witches enjoy in the same way ordinary people enjoy sherry.

'Let the games begin,' Mordonna cried, and as she did so the stadium gates opened and the first competitor from last year's ultra-ultra-seriously-long-distance marathon ran into the stadium. His arms raised high in the air, the winner, Fleetwood Flood (second cousin), did a final lap of the stadium and collapsed at Mordonna's feet.

In the three hundred and sixty-five days since the race had begun, Fleetwood had covered eighteen galaxies and six parallel universes. He had run, swum, cycled, tangoed, teleported and flown through wind and rain, night and day and Belgium. He'd had nine

---

[34] *Meaning Mordonna's sunglasses, because as everyone knows, one glance into Mordonna's eyes and you fall madly in love with her.*

total body transplants, been married twice and even learnt to ask for a cup of tea in Belgian.

As he was lowered into the winner's coffin, Mordonna placed the gold medal round his neck and the spectators cheered.[35]

Mordonna went back to her seat and the field and track events began.

Traditionally the relay race was the first event. Witches and wizards could never understand why people would want to run round a track handing each other a stick, so they changed the rules slightly. Quicklime's relay was much more exciting. Instead of a stick they used a poisonous snake and the point of the race was not to take the snake from someone else but to do your best *not* to take it. The winner was the team with the least number of dead members. The Floods always won this event because of their highly developed team techniques. No equipment or special clothing was allowed, such as barbecue tongs

---

[35] *It would be three days before the second place competitor reached the stadium and by then everyone would have gone home and it was the school holidays.*

or leather gloves, but there was nothing to stop you using your own natural gifts. So Merlinmary always led their team out and simply electrocuted the snake. As it was against the rules to kill the snakes, Satanella then grabbed the dead animal from Merlinmary and ran round the track shaking it violently in her teeth so everyone thought it was still alive. The twins then followed, using the snake as a skipping rope, before Winchflat slipped it one of his special iSnakezombie pills that made it kind of appear to be still alive just long enough for him to carry it past the finish line.

In fact, the Floods won every event apart from the gymnastic dancing, where you jump around on a big mat waving a stick with a ribbon on the end. They found it impossible to compete in that without collapsing in laughter. And they *never* competed in the high diving because, like all sensible people, they didn't do drugs.

Finally, it was time for the day's most popular event: the three-legged race.

The Floods tossed a coin to see who would leave their legs behind and then they tied themselves

together with Merlinmary sitting on Winchflat's shoulders and Satanella jammed in between the twins.

Unlike the other single runners, who had grown an extra leg for the day, Howard Tiny had had himself photocopied. He had lain sideways on the photocopier so only one of his legs got copied.

'You should do this more often, seventy-two, seventy-three, seventy-four,' said Howard's photocopy. 'With two heads we could count bigger numbers, ninety-eight.'

'Yes, and there'd always be one of us

The Three-Legged race attracts many strange entries

there to pull the sock out of the other's mouth, one hundred and one, two, three, four!' said the original Howard. 'I'll ask Mum if you can stay.'

Radius Leg, the sports master, had never been present on a single sports day. He had spent more than half his career in traction or intensive care under Matron's watchful eye. This sports day he was still hibernating under a snowdrift. So, as she did every year, Matron had brought her Radius Leg clone out of her spare parts cupboard.[36]

'Three, two, one, BANG!' shouted the Radius Leg clone, and the race began. As always there were several children who had grown their extra legs back to front. They stayed at the starting line going in circles until the runners came round for the second lap and knocked them flying. Howard Tiny, who was really tiny, got about halfway round the track and sat down on the grass.

---

[36] *Matron had clones for every member of staff, including herself. They had not been created using Winchflat's new Special 3D Photocopier, but by an older, much more dangerous system that often produced clones that were nothing like the originals.*

'I've always wanted to count to two hundred and forty-seven,' he said to his photocopy.

'That's my favourite number too,' said the half-Howard.

After seven laps there were only three teams left in the race. The Floods began the final lap with Bypass Noble, who had managed to grow a third leg with a big spring in it, very close behind them. Two laps back, a small figure hidden inside a paper bag ran as fast as his little legs would carry him. It was Charlie – formerly known as The Toad – and the paper bag was to make sure Orkward Warlock wouldn't recognise him. The trouble was, no one had put any eye holes in the paper bag and Charlie kept getting lost. Also, the extra leg Matron had lent him from her spare parts cupboard was the wrong size and he kept tripping over it. He finished fifteen minutes after the other two teams, but still got the bronze medal.

Orkward sat on a rock outside the treasure cave and looked down into the stadium far below him. Even from this far away he could hear the sounds coming from the crowd. They were sounds that Orkward hated and despised, the sounds of people having a good time and being happy.

He would teach them.

He would give them a new sound, the sound of five revolting Floods children exploding into a billion little pieces that even Matron wouldn't be able to reassemble. As he watched, Narled trundled across the grass towards the medal winners' podium. The Floods, as Orkward had predicted, had won the three-legged race and were standing there looking

disgustingly happy, waiting to get their billionth gold medals. As Satanella ran round the stadium doing a lap of honour, the hatred Orkward Warlock felt for the Floods grew so big he felt as if his head would explode. It was bad enough that they won everything, got all the gold stars, had more friends than anyone else, had the most beautiful mother in the entire universe and just looked so horribly pleased with themselves, but now they had made him get a pounding headache too. As Merlinmary held her hands high in the air and the

entire stadium cheered when she sent fabulous bolts of lightning soaring up into the clouds, Orkward felt the veins on his neck throbbing louder and louder like a bass drum. Blood began to trickle down his nose, blood that no longer tasted sweet on his tongue but was as bitter as his soul.

Narled disappeared beneath the stand and re-emerged a few seconds later. Orkward took out a remote control box from his backpack and switched it on. The red light on it started to flash. It throbbed like a heartbeat and Orkward felt his thumb twitch in excitement. His mouth went dry and his own heart began to beat in time with the red button. He felt faint with excitement.

Ten, nine, eight …

Professor Throat walked forward carrying the medals.

Seven, six, five, four …

The Professor reached down and pinned the first medal to Satanella Flood's collar. She wagged her tail with such enthusiasm that she threw herself off the podium.

Three, two …

Orkward pressed the button.

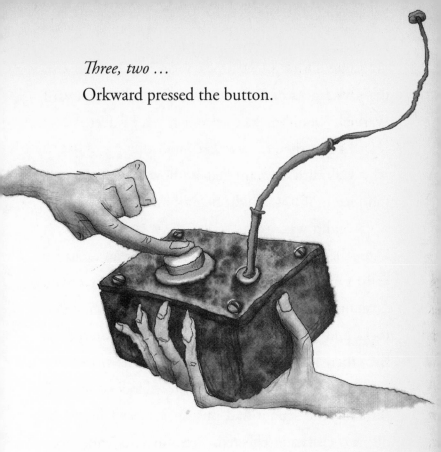

Time seemed to stop. The wind that always ran down the valley stood still. The split second seemed like an hour. The blood on Orkward's tongue, though as bitter as before, now tasted like fine wine, and in that last split second he realised who his true father was.

He, Orkward Warlock, was the devil's child.

He, Orkward Warlock, was son and heir to the dark forces of the underworld and he, Orkward Warlock, would make everyone fall at his feet.

Except then the world exploded.

Orkward was amazed by how loud it was. It sounded as if it was right behind him.

And it was.

The mouth of the cave erupted in an amazing ball of fire. Narled's treasure trove burst out of the cave in all directions. It flattened trees, shattered rocks and blew Orkward Warlock into more pieces than there are grains of sand in the whole world.[37]

Down in the stadium the crowd looked up and, thinking the school had put on a special fireworks display, everyone cheered. Seconds later, hundreds of wonderful things began to rain down on them. Seventy-three iPods, countless gold coins, seven hundred and nine lost buttons, bits of Lego, ballpoint pens, missing pieces of jigsaw puzzles, shoes, and

---

[37] *Not including a seventy-mile beach in north Queensland. If you add that in, then there were fifteen more grains of sand than grains of Orkward Warlock.*

twelve thousand pages of missing homework covered the playing field and half the valley. In the fourth year common room, twelve gold crowns, three French hens and a partridge in a pear sauce flew out of the fireplace as the explosion shot out of the back of the cave and down the secret tunnel Merlinmary had discovered.

'Wow, that was some firework,' said Nerlin Flood as a diamond the size of a chicken's egg landed in his lap.

A small china doll flew through the window into Orkward's old room and landed on the bed.

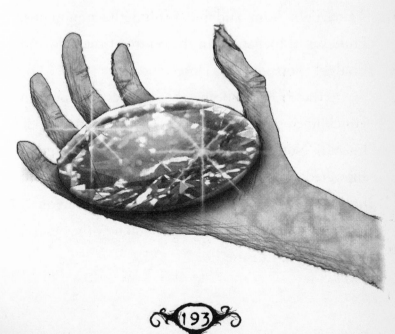

'Beryl, is that, like, you?' said The Mirror.

'No,' said the china doll. 'She got broken years ago.'

'Oh,' said The Mirror sadly.

'Just kidding,' said Beryl, turning back into a seriously gorgeous girl.

'So why haven't I changed back?'

'In a minute, in a minute,' said Beryl, staring at her reflection. 'I just need to fix my hair.'

As daylight went and hid behind the mountains, Professor Throat stood in the centre of the field and brought sports day to a close.

'These have been the greatest games in Quicklime's seven hundred and fifty glorious years,' he said. 'Not just because of the great explosion that showered everyone with gold and diamonds, but because of the great team spirit shown by everyone.'

No one believed him. They all knew the best bit had been the treasure.

'Of course,' the Professor concluded, 'being the seven hundred and fifty-*first* year, a number of great significance in the world of magic, next year's sports day will be even greater ...'

Charlie, no longer a toad, was reunited with his parents, who felt so proud of his bronze medal and so incredibly guilty at how badly they had treated him that they spoilt him rotten for the rest of his life. He had a different iPod and Playstation in every room of the house, fourteen stunning girlfriends, a massive plasma TV, his own go-kart racing track and a special secret place in the dark forest where he could visit the little handbags whenever he wanted to.

So that Orkward Warlock wouldn't go down in history as a total failure, a new combined high, low, far and wide jump event was created and Orkward

was awarded a lifetime achievement gold medal as the person who had jumped the highest, the lowest and the furthest all at the same time. But even then, his parents still wouldn't have anything to do with him.[38]

The Floods didn't need a special happy ending, because their lives were just about perfect anyway. Their only worry was being totally unable to think of anything that could make their lives any better.

Back home on the first evening of the school holidays, the whole family sat on the back verandah drinking warm blood slurpies as the ice-cold moon

---

[38] *Come on, Orkward Warlock was vile. He doesn't deserve a happy ending. Anyway, how could his parents have anything to do with him when he was blown up into a million, billion little pieces. Surely that's way too many pieces to ever be put back together again. Or is it?*

And it's not true that Orkward was the devil's son. His dad really was the milkman, and a milkman disguise is much too ordinary for the Prince of Darkness. Or is it?

rose over the trees and sparkled on all the gold medals the children had won.

'I think,' said Mordonna, 'that was the best sports day ever.'

'Absolutely,' everyone agreed. 'At least until next year's.'

'I'm not going back to the retirement cave,' said Alzhammer the dragon. 'I mean, what's the point? I'll just get off to sleep again and it'll be time to come here again for next year's sports day.'

'But what about your passengers?' someone asked.

'They're as old as me,' said Alzhammer. 'We'll all stay here.'

Which was how Quicklime College became the first school in history to have classes on false teeth maintenance and how to crochet lumpy things.

The School Song

Oh Quicklime's dark and evil
It is to thee we sing
You fill us full of magic
And help our dreams take wing.

You give us timeless power
And secret ancient curses
You teach us timeless potions
And how to service hearses.

Quicklime's, ancient Quicklime's
Long may your darkness reign
And may you bring the long, long dead
Back to life again.

Oh Quicklime's dark and evil
You turn the day to night
You show us how to sleepwalk
And set our beds alight.

You give us all the magic ways
From centuries gone by
And the secret recipe
For making phoenix pie.

200

```
Quicklime's, ancient Quicklime's
  Long may your darkness rule
And may you bring the long,long dead
  To visit our great school.
```

And so on for thirty-three more verses.*

---

* Or thirty-five more if you include the two really rude verses
that have been banned by the Parents Committee, who know
how bad the verses are from singing them when they were at
Quicklime's.

The Weird and Mystical Mobius Strip

Or how to draw on both sides of a piece of paper without taking your pen off the paper.

1 - Take a strip of paper about 20 cm long and 2 cm wide.

2 - Twist it once.

3 - Keep the twist in the paper and tape the two ends together.

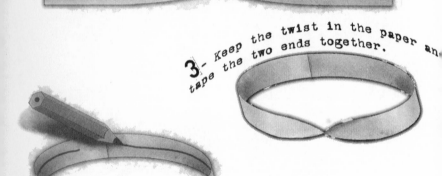

4 - Draw a line along the middle of the paper and don't take the pencil off the paper until you get back to the start.

5 - Try to paint the front and back two different colours.

6 - Cut the strip along the pencil line.

As you can see a Mobius Strip is very weird. This is how Winchflat's friend Eric Ordinaire got trapped inside the internet.

How to Make YOur Very Own
Gristleball

Very few of you will have access to a giant Patagonian ballworm, so here is an easy way to make a substitute gristleball from two simple ingredients.

You will need:
- 3 million rubber bands
- 2 pints of dragon dribble.

Simply make a huge ball out of the rubber bands, coating each layer with dragon dribble as you go. Then leave it in a festering ditch for a month to ripen. (If you can't get dragon dribble, you can use anything that leaks out of your baby brother or sister.)

The
Quicklime
College
Teachers
Files

PROFESSOR THROAT
NB, PDF, PS
HSC(Ghent)

Professor Throat is the fifteenth Throat to hold the job of headmaster at Quicklime's. He has been unable to find or manufacture someone strange enough to want to marry him and so when he retires, he will be the last Throat to run the school. There are plans to dig up his grandfather and put him back in the job.

Matron has been secretly in love with Professor Throat for years, but her love is so secret that even she doesn't know about it.

The Professor is a fair man (except for his left foot, which is actually very dark), and generally loved by one and all.

His best friend is a Belgian Mongoose called Rembrandt, who lives in the dark folds of the Professor's gown and only comes out during a full moon.

PREBENDER GLORIOUS
Invisibility

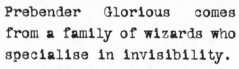

Prebender Glorious comes from a family of wizards who specialise in invisibility.

Because of this brilliant talent, PG's relatives are behind some of the greatest and most daring unsolved crimes in history.

PG himself has a defective gene which makes his invisibility totally unpredictable. It means that he might suddenly appear at a very bad moment. Because of this he has been unable to enjoy the great rewards the rest of his family have earned. The world of crime's loss, however, has been Quicklime College's gain. His lack of control over his own invisibility make his classes very entertaining.

RADIUS LEG
Sport with Pain

Radius Leg was originally built out of bricks and changed into a PE teacher with a special spell.

Because of his origins as a building, he has a very high pain threshold, though not as high as he thinks. During his teaching career he has followed a very strict training regimen which has resulted in the carefully planned breaking of every single bone in his body.

DOCTOR MORDANT
Genetic Engineering

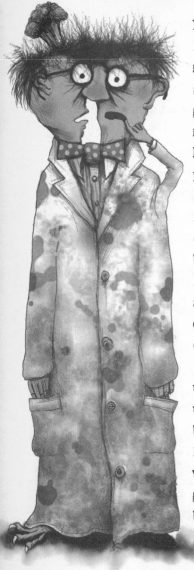

Doctor Mordant is, quite literally, a self-made man. Beginning life as a small blob of bacteria growing on a piece of mouldy camembert, Doctor Mordant began the exciting path of evolution when a live electric wire came into contact with the cheese. In a matter of hours, he had grown a few legs. A day later his arms appeared, and by the end of the week he was a fully qualified school teacher.

His evolution continues to this day as he is unable to decide exactly how many legs he would like to end up with, and what colour the broccoli growing out of his spare head should be.

MADEMOISELLE FIFI la VENUS Elocution and Howling

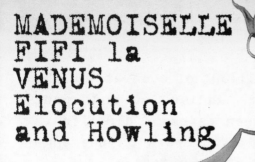

All the male teachers and most of the boys at Quicklime's are in love with Fifi la Venus, and who wouldn't adore her delicate wings and armour-piercing scream?

She's the only person to have shattered every single window in the Sydney Opera House while singing in Moscow. At night she roosts on a nest of phoenix feathers in a special tree in the school quadrangle.

MATRON

Matron was built out of concrete in the same factory as Radius Leg and spent the first fifteen years of her life as a shed full of lawnmowers on the edge of Quicklime's playing fields.

Her two nurses, Romeo and Juliet, lived in a nest inside her roof until one night, during the greatest storm of the century, they were struck by an incredible bolt of lightning which actually had nothing to do with the storm but was caused by Romeo eating through a power cable.

This coincided with the old Matron *actually* being struck by lightning so Matron and her two nurses were given the job.

Over the years since then Matron has invented and collected an awesome and scary dispensary of spells and medicines.

Dr. Phlegm's Horrendous Cure-all

MISS PHYLLIS
Special Breeds

Miss Phyllis has the unique distinction of being the only person to have both won a top award (Best in Breed - Cuddly Pet Class) at Cruft's famous dog show and been a judge in the same show.

The Special Breeds children adore her. Not just because she is a kind, caring person, or because she can cook seventeen amazing dinners out of nothing more than a rat, two sheep's ears and a tin of dog food,* and not because she never makes them learn boring things like Maths and Belgian, but because she is absolutely brilliant at catching a red rubber ball in mid-air.

---

* *You might have actually seen Miss Phyllis on her famous TV show* The Mouth-Watering Mongrel.

AUBERGINE WEALTH
Economics and Other Forms of Burglary

Starting with a mere five million dollars given to him by his grandfather on his fifth birthday, by using his natural talents, Aubergine is now worth more than Belgium and Italy added together.

He enjoys the finer things in life, such as expensive wines, platinum wands and Gucci broomsticks. He dines on corn-fed endangered species and even the gravy stains on his dicky* come from Harrods and were made by a top chef.

He teaches at Quicklime's because as an ex-student he wants to give something back.

---

* Don't be rude. A dicky is a false shirt front worn to keep your shirt clean. Like a posh bib for grown-ups.

THE OTHER TEACHERS

There are a lot more teachers at Quicklime College and other staff, like Narled and Doorlock, who keep the school running smoothly. Unfortunately we don't have enough time or space to meet such wonderful people as Arkforth Prenderfoot, who teaches dead languages (for dead students), or Geraldine Saltwater, who teaches Underwater French, or Diabolus Prawn, the Underwater Dancing teacher, who is only part-time because the rest of the time he is a bookcase.

Maybe in a future book we will return to Quicklime's and meet the legendary Lord Algernon Tuppence-Change, who teaches sinew weaving, and Sugar-Cane Molasses, the world famous tango dancer.

Did YOU Miss THiS?

THE FLOODS 1

Avoid becoming a sad unloved loser by rushing out
and buying a copy NOW!!!

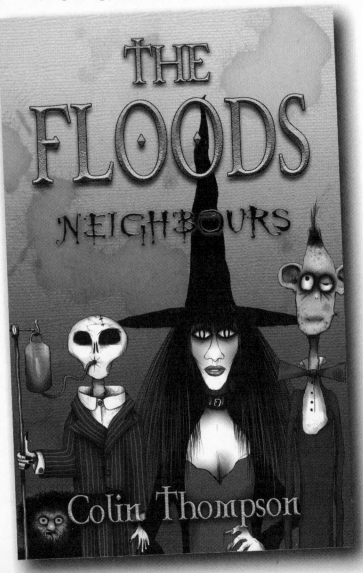

THE FLOODS 1
NEIGHBOURS

Everybody needs good neighbours …

The Floods aren't like other families – for a start, they're all witches and wizards. And they weren't made in the traditional way like you or me. Some of Nerlin and Mordonna Flood's six eldest children were made in the cellar, using an ancient recipe book and a very big turbocharged wand. The youngest child, Betty, is a normal, pretty little girl – but her attempts at magic never go the way she plans.

The next-door neighbours should have known better than to annoy a family of witches and wizards. But they did, and they're about to find out what the Floods do to bad neighbours.

ComInG iN

Late 2006
THE FLOODS 3

HOME AND AWAY

The cover's not actually top secret. I just haven't drawn it yet.